T0090508

The
TABLE OF ELEMENTS
and the
SPACE STATION
of
SRILVAKOR

BOOK ONE

Noah Cannon

WESTBOW
PRESS®
A DIVISION OF THOMAS NELSON
& ZONDERVAN

WestBow Press books may be ordered through booksellers or by contacting:

WestBow Press
A Division of Thomas Nelson & Zondervan
1663 Liberty Drive
Bloomington, IN 47403
www.westbowpress.com
844-714-3454

Because of the dynamic nature of the Internet, any web addresses or
links contained in this book may have changed since publication and
may no longer be valid. The views expressed in this work are solely those
of the author and do not necessarily reflect the views of the publisher,
and the publisher hereby disclaims any responsibility for them.

Any people depicted in stock imagery provided by Getty Images are
models, and such images are being used for illustrative purposes only.
Certain stock imagery © Getty Images.

Edited by Rebecca LuElla Miller

Scripture quotations marked KJV are from the Holy Bible, King James
Version (Authorized Version). First published in 1611. Quoted from the KJV
Classic Reference Bible, Copyright © 1983 by The Zondervan Corporation.

ISBN: 979-8-3850-1674-7 (sc)
ISBN: 979-8-3850-1676-1 (hc)
ISBN: 979-8-3850-1675-4 (e)

Library of Congress Control Number: 2024900801

Print information available on the last page.

WestBow Press rev. date: 01/17/2024

For Dad—
A great editor and an amazing father

For Paul—
One of my favorite authors

Contents

CHAPTER ONE

M R. STARCLUSTER'S HEART was racing like a marathon runner. He hadn't expected anything like this to happen. Why would he? He had just seen his son that morning. What possibly could have happened in so short a time? But there he was, briskly following a doctor down the barren hospital hall after getting a call saying that his son had been in an accident.

"Is Steven all right?" Mr. Starcluster asked the doctor. "What happened?"

"Paramedics recovered him, the rest of his class, and their bus driver buried underneath the wreckage of their vehicle in the Presidio," said the doctor. "They all survived. We're going to run more tests on him and his friend, Miss Adams, tomorrow before they can be cleared to go home."

"What are their injuries?" Mr. Starcluster pressed, riddled with concern.

"Mild concussions, cuts, and some bruises, but no broken bones," the doctor answered.

Mr. Starcluster sighed with relief. Sure, it was still bad, but at least Steven and his friend were alive, and their injuries weren't as long-lasting as he feared.

"What caused the accident?"

"I'm sorry to say I don't know," said the doctor. "The details haven't been released."

Then, she and Mr. Starcluster reached a door at the end of the hall. The doctor put a finger to her lips before she let him enter. "Stay as long as you like, but please keep your voice down," she said. "It's important that he rests."

Mr. Starcluster nodded as his shaking hand grasped the door handle and opened the door at a turtle's pace. Inside were two beds. One was empty and the other was occupied by his fifteen-year-old son Steven, his only child. He was wearing a pale blue hospital gown and did not look his best, but not just because his head and right arm were covered in bandages. Mr. Starcluster could see flashes of trauma in his son's eyes, as though he was watching something scary and depressing.

Mr. Starcluster hobbled on his cane over to the side of the bed. "Steven, what happened?"

Steven murmured unintelligibly. He didn't look his father in the eye, but Mr. Starcluster caught a glimpse of tears forming in his own.

"It's going to be OK, kiddo," said Mr. Starcluster.

"No, it's not," said Steven shakily.

Mr. Starcluster was puzzled. He was *beyond* puzzled. The suspense was consuming him. He needed to know what was going on or he might go mad. "What happened?" he asked again.

*   *   *

EARLIER THAT DAY

Steven Starcluster turned off his alarm the moment it went off at seven o'clock that morning. He had woken up about an hour earlier and could not get back to sleep, no matter how hard he tried. He was much too excited to even *think* about sleeping.

He jumped out of bed and hurried over to his wall calendar. It was Wednesday the tenth—the day he had been looking forward to for the past month—the day he and his history class from Pine Tree High were going on a field trip to the brand-new Table of Elements Museum and Memorial.

The Table of Elements were a team of four superheroes who wore armored suits which gave them powers based on the periodic table, hence the chemical portion of their name. For nearly nine years, they protected San Francisco from villains and criminals of many sorts and were loved by just about everyone in the city. Steven and his friend Brooklyn were huge fans of their work. They thought of them the way people thought of George Washington or Abraham Lincoln. Steven even dreamed of being a member as a kid until he learned in school that three of the four members were deceased, and the sole survivor hadn't been seen since retirement. Though disappointed that he never met the Table of Elements, Steven was still excited to visit the new museum.

After doing some pushups, Steven read his devotional and Bible before getting dressed, making sure to wear his *Table of Elements* sweatshirt. After brushing his teeth, he hurried downstairs to make breakfast, but his dad, Boaz, had already beat him to it.

"Slow down, speedy!" said Boaz heartily as he pulled four square waffles out of the waffle iron and onto a plate with a spatula. "School doesn't start for an hour."

"I know, I know," said Steven, smiling as though Christmas had come early. "I'm just so excited!"

"Really? I couldn't tell," Boaz joked before turning off the waffle iron. "I've read good reviews about the museum. I'm sure you and your friends will have a blast."

"Just one," said Steven. Though still in a good mood, the mention of him only having one other friend began to drip like a leaky faucet into his happy demeanor. "I'm still not exactly Mr. Popular."

Boaz hobbled over to the oak counter and set the plate of waffles down before Steven. "You're a great kid, all the same," said Boaz kindly.

"Thanks," said Steven, getting up and hugging his dad. "And you're the best dad in the world! Always will be."

"I'd like that in writing, please," Boaz teased, "in case I need leverage from you."

The father and son sat at the counter and ate their breakfast together.

Boaz was tall and burly, with a round face, a goatee, and curly orange hair that was graying in places. Even though he was only forty-three, he had to walk with a cane because of a serious leg injury he received over a decade ago. Steven was about the average height for someone his age. He was a clean-cut young gentleman with short, wavy orange hair, a heart-shaped face, rosy cheeks, dimples, and watery blue eyes.

Boaz and Steven lived at 345 Stockton Street in the iconic West Coast city of San Francisco. Their building was thirty-six stories high, and they got to live in the penthouse because Boaz was the building's cofounder and manager. The establishment was called BRCA Apartments, named after the first initials of Boaz and the other three founders: Robert, Charlotte, and Andrea.

Boaz's penthouse was the perfect apartment to live in. It had two stories, three comfy bedrooms, and a breathtaking view of Union Square from the sitting room. The smooth walls, painted in a cozy cream color, went with the polished dark oak floor like ham went with eggs. The entire interior, designed by Boaz, had a simple yet rustic design. Steven loved living in the city, but the warm down-to-earth environment of the penthouse was always refreshing to come home to after a long day out in the concrete jungle.

"Are you sure you don't want to go to the museum?" Steven asked. "You can meet me there."

"Sorry, kiddo, I have a meeting today," said Boaz.

Though disappointed, Steven remained positive. He understood how important his father's job was. "All right," he said nonchalantly. "Well, I'll take lots of pictures for you!"

"I look forward to seeing them," said Boaz.

Steven finished his breakfast and hugged his dad goodbye before Boaz headed upstairs to get dressed for work. Steven wasn't a fan of the fact that his dad had an upstairs bedroom with his leg impairment, but Boaz insisted that the exercise was good for him.

Steven threw his blue backpack over his shoulders before heading out the door and locking it behind him. Still buzzing with anticipation, he rode the elevator, which was directly across the hall from the penthouse, down to the lobby.

When the door opened on the first floor, Steven found himself face to face with a girl his age. She was a couple of inches shorter than he was and had dark brown eyes. Her wavy, armpit-length brown hair had caramel streaks, like raindrops down a window, flowing through it. She was staring directly at Steven with eyes as wide as Frisbees and a creepy nightmare-inducing grin. She was Steven's best friend, Brooklyn Adams.

Brooklyn standing right outside the elevator was an unexpected shock for Steven. He yelped the second he saw her.

Brooklyn laughed. "That never gets old," she said. She had a warm laid-back voice that oozed "cool" in every way. It helped that *she* was plenty cool herself.

She was wearing a black and white checkered flannel, a gray *Table of Elements* themed T-shirt, skinny black jeans, white high-top shoes, and five different bracelets. Her skateboard was sticking out of the top of her black backpack which she wore loosely over her shoulders.

Brooklyn lived two floors below Steven and Boaz and liked to surprise the former whenever he rode down the elevator. However, since she didn't have a set date for when she did this, Steven was hardly prepared for her alarming greetings. The one time he *did* prepare himself, when he was twelve, he jumped out and yelled *"Roar!"* when the doors opened, and unintentionally caused a lady to gasp, jump, and spill her coffee on her shirt that said, "Coffee Makes Me Scream For Joy." And while there was indeed a whole lot of screaming, Steven was pretty sure joy wasn't the emotion behind it.

"At least she understood and didn't get all mad or anything," Brooklyn said when he told her.

"Yeah, I was thankful for that," Steven had said. "She was actually pretty nice."

"Let's get going," said Brooklyn. "We don't want to miss the field trip."

"No, we do not!" Steven agreed, enunciating each word.

Steven and Brooklyn passed through the lobby and headed out the front door. From there, they turned left and headed north on Stockton Street. Despite living in a big, busy city, their school was only a couple of blocks away, on the corner of Stockton and Pine, and so they walked there and back together every day.

"How's your dad?" Steven asked.

"He's good," said Brooklyn.

"Has he solved any mysteries or uncovered a secret villain plot or anything?"

Brooklyn rolled her eyes. "He's the chief of police, not a detective," she reminded Steven. "But he has been leading a team to try to apprehend those drive-by thieves."

"The convertible gang?" Steven assumed.

"Yeah, that's them," Brooklyn confirmed.

"He's a great cop," said Steven. "I'm sure he'll catch them in no time."

After history class, their teacher, Mr. Williamson, collected the students' field trip permission slips before they lined up outside to get on the school bus. Steven stood behind Brooklyn in line, and the two eagerly discussed what they most looked forward to seeing at the museum.

"We've got to get a picture in front of the uniform displays," said Steven. "Dibs on standing next to Helium's suit!"

"Will they have the Regnier?" Brooklyn asked, referring to the Table of Elements' famous vehicle. It could transform from a spaceship into a car with a lever pull and a button push.

"No, but I wish they did," Steven answered, remembering something he read. "To this day, people still don't know where it is, but I think the museum has a replica or something to take pictures with. I think that still sounds cool."

"Aw, what would you know about 'cool,' Starcluster?" a nasty voice sneered from behind.

Steven cringed. He didn't need to turn around to know whose voice that was. It belonged to Eddie Macaron, a bully who was in the same history class as Steven and Brooklyn. He was about a head taller than Steven, square-jawed, and muscular, with curly strawberry-blond hair. He had cut in line so he could pick on Steven, who said nothing as Eddie laughed spitefully with his buddies.

"Hey, Starcluster!" Eddie barked. "I'm talking to you!"

"Hey, Eddie," said Steven coolly.

Eddie might have gotten under his skin numerous times, but Steven kept praying that God would help him stay calm and not give in to his anger.

"Are you and your girlfriend ready to nerd out over costumes and junk?" Eddie scoffed.

"She's not my girlfriend," said Steven, swallowing down his frustration like a disgusting medicine. "And I think the Table of Elements deserve more respect. They saved the city countless times."

"Oh, no!" Eddie exclaimed in a voice filled with fake fear, turning to his friends behind him. "You hear that, guys? *The Table of Elements deserve more respect!* Let's paint their names on our shirts and drool over their precious costumes!"

Steven took a deep breath, struggling not to clench his fists.

"Please leave me alone," he told Eddie as calmly as he could.

"'Please leave me alone?' " Eddie repeated. "What are you, a boy scout?"

He flicked Steven on the forehead.

Brooklyn immediately threw herself between them.

"Hey! You heard him," she said firmly. "Leave him alone, or I'll tell Principal Sanchez."

"Bah! I'm not scared of Principal Sanchez!" said Eddie.

"Is that so?" a sharp female voice interjected.

To Steven's relief, it was Principal Sanchez. She was tall and slender, with a stern face and blonde hair tied into a bun. She was crossing her arms, and whether you knew her or not, you could tell she was not a person to get on the wrong side of.

Eddie stopped taunting Steven and Brooklyn immediately. His face showed fear for a fraction of a second until he resorted to a look of annoyed boredom.

"I've already told you, Mr. Macaron," said Principal Sanchez calmly but strictly. "If you touch Steven one more time, you'll have detention for the rest of the week. Do I make myself clear?"

Eddie grumbled. "Yes, Principal Sanchez."

"Good. Now why don't you and your friends return to your proper spot in line?" said Principal Sanchez, her arms still crossed. "Miss Ackerman told me you took her spot."

Steven glanced back to find Lucy Ackerman, who didn't look very happy about being cut in line.

"Yes, ma'am," said Eddie. "Let's go, guys."

He and the others shuffled back behind Lucy.

"Thank you, Mrs. Sanchez," said Steven.

The principal's stern demeanor morphed into a friendly smile. "No problem. Let me know if he causes you any more trouble." She told him and Brooklyn to have fun on the trip before turning around and heading back inside the school.

By this time, Steven and Brooklyn had finally reached the front of the line. They entered the bus and sat in the middle.

"Thanks for sticking up for me," Steven told Brooklyn as he sat down.

Brooklyn sat beside him.

"Eddie gets under my skin," Steven continued. "I know the Bible says to love your enemies, but it's just so, so hard."

"But you controlled your temper, and that's good," Brooklyn pointed out.

"I know but ..." Steven stopped. After a moment he asked, "Brooklyn, have you ever wondered why we're so close?"

Brooklyn looked appalled that he had even asked.

"Where's *that* coming from?"

"We're so different," said Steven. "You're the embodiment of cool. You skateboard like a pro and rock at every video game there is. I'm not that talented at *anything*, and I just stick to books and stuff."

"Don't think like that, dude. You're plenty talented and plenty cool to *me,* and I couldn't ask for a better best friend."

Steven smiled slightly. "Thanks," he said again. "You're right. I'll try to ignore him. 'Me and my girlfriend.' " He chuckled. *"Girlfriend."*

Brooklyn chuckled, too. "Yeah ..." she said as though she was forcing herself to sound amused. "Your ... *girlfriend."*

"Yeah ..." Steven agreed, trying not to blush.

There was an awkward silence between them, but it ended almost as soon as it had started. Everyone had finally entered the bus and had taken their seats. The driver closed the doors and pulled out of the parking lot. The field trip had begun at last.

CHAPTER TWO

THE TABLE OF Elements Museum and Memorial was in the Presidio of San Francisco, a beautiful green area in the city's northwest region, home to many historical sights. After entering the Presidio, the bus turned left off Washington Boulevard onto Kobbe Avenue, the museum's street. Steven and Brooklyn stared in awe. Their faces formed smiles of uncontrollable excitement when they saw the museum for the first time in person. It was white and light gray and made of stone and marble. It was smaller than the Academy of Sciences and the De Young Museum, but it was still an impressive sight.

A magnificent stone fountain had been erected in front of the entrance, with stone statues of the four Table of Elements members standing heroically with their fists on their hips and their backs straight.

Mr. Williamson, who had driven there in his car instead of

taking the bus, made some final announcements to his students outside the museum.

"Remember everyone, we are here to listen and learn," he said. "Pay attention to the guide and raise your hand if you have any questions. *Real* questions."

He gave Eddie Macaron and his goons a pointed look.

As Mr. Williamson concluded his speech, the museum doors opened, and the tour guide exited through them and approached the group. She was a short and friendly-looking old woman, with plump cheeks and silver hair.

"Welcome to the Table of Elements Museum and Memorial!" she announced in a voice that made Steven feel even more excited than he already was. "If you'll please follow me, we will begin our tour. But first, are there any questions?"

Brooklyn was one of the few who raised their hand. To her and Steven's delight, the guide selected her.

"Have you ever met the Table of Elements?" Brooklyn asked.

The guide smiled. Steven assumed she was driving down Memory Lane.

"Indeed, I did," she cheerfully replied. "They saved my family and me from a fire many years ago. It was an unforgettable experience."

Steven grinned. He was very intrigued that their guide had been rescued by the Table of Elements themselves. To him, it gave the tour a more personal feel. He hoped the guide had more stories to tell during their time at the museum.

The inside of the museum was even more impressive than the outside. It was light, bright, and pearly white, as though it had been carved from a cloud. Paintings and enlarged photographs of the Table of Elements and their incredible feats were posted on the walls. Numerous trinkets and artifacts stood on display behind glass. Steven and Brooklyn swung their heads in all directions as they moved with their class through the building, trying to take in everything at once.

The guide showed them many things, including the life-size Regnier replica that Steven and Brooklyn had discussed before arriving.

"As you might know," said the guide, "the Regnier was built and operated by the Table of Elements over twenty years ago. On land, the vehicle could go from zero to sixty in three-point-five seconds. In space, its top speed was eighteen lightyears per hour. To this day, its N-122 hyperdrive remains one of the fastest models ever built."

Mr. Williamson and some students took photos of the replica spaceship, including Steven and Brooklyn, who took selfies together before deciding to take individual shots.

Steven stood back to snap a photo of Brooklyn standing in front of the ship when Eddie jumped out of nowhere and screamed in his ear, causing Steven to yelp and drop his phone. Eddie appeared so suddenly that Brooklyn didn't have time to warn her friend. By the time Steven spun around, Eddie was already hurrying off, laughing mischievously with his goons.

Steven burned red with anger as he bent down and retrieved his phone.

"Are you OK?" Brooklyn asked.

"*No,*" Steven growled in a hushed voice.

"Say a prayer and take a deep breath," Brooklyn comforted.

Steven took her advice as they continued their tour with the rest of the group. He asked God to give him self-control and to help him control his anger. By the time they reached the next exhibit, he was already in a better mood, much to Brooklyn's delight.

The next exhibit was truly special. All four of the Table

of Elements' superhero uniforms were displayed behind thick glass cases. Despite being made up of protective armor, the suits looked very slim, almost skintight, and not bulky whatsoever. The plates were broken into multiple tiny pieces over all the main muscles to allow flexibility and freedom of movement, as Steven remembered reading.

The suit in the middle belonged to Helium. He had been the team leader and was the only member still alive. The suit came with an armored cowl, separate from the uniform, which covered the wearer's entire head and face except for the mouth and top of the head. Steven humorously assumed that this was so Helium's hair could flow in the wind to make himself look cooler than he already was.

The bodysuit was silver, and the armor plates and cowl were royal blue. A bulky black utility belt was buckled around the waist with a pouch on either side, and a pearly-white, round emblem with a black outline was in the middle of the suit's chest. In the emblem's center was the periodic symbol for helium: "He."

The other suits were identical in design, except they had different symbols and colors. All the blue portions of Helium's armor had been substituted with either white, yellow, or purple.

The white uniform had been Silicon's, whose symbol was "Si," the yellow suit was Lithium's, bearing the symbol "Li," and the purple suit was Beryllium's, the symbol of which was "Be."

Despite the color differences, all four utility belts were the same ebony color. Helium and Lithium had been men, and Silicon and Beryllium, women. According to the guide, the four of them had been best friends even before they had become superheroes, though their identities were still a secret to the public.

"More impressive than the suits are the Element Blasters,"

said the guide, leading them to a TV screen on the wall beside them.

The guide turned on the screen with a remote she had. The TV showed a 3-D rendering of one of the Table of Elements' Blasters. The guide pointed to the top of the suit's forearm, where a thin, little pipe was attached. After pressing another button on the remote, the top of the Blaster on the screen opened up, revealing a complex jungle of wires, gears, and screws. In the center was a small, rectangular metal box, no bigger than a battery you'd find at a convenience store.

"This is the suit's generator," the guide explained. "Inside is a sample of whichever element the suit represented. When the wearer used his or her powers, this device would amplify the element's abilities and project it through the nozzle on top of the Blaster."

Steven might have known this fact by heart, but that didn't stop him from being fully immersed in the guide's words. She then went into full detail about the powers of the Table of Elements. As she described each ability, footage of each Table of Elements member in action appeared on the screen in order of whose power she discussed.

"Helium's iconic Helium Boots allowed him to fly at incredible speeds, his top speed being five hundred miles per hour. With the press of a button on his technological glove, helium would spray out of the soles of his boots. His Element Blasters were *also* capable of spraying helium, powerful enough to make an entire tank hover a hundred feet above the ground. Like the rest of the team, his Element Blasters were activated by pressing the button on his index finger with his thumb."

A student raised his hand.

"How long would the helium last?"

"It depended on how much was sprayed," answered the

guide. "If Helium kept the object in a 'tractor beam,' so to speak, then it could have been suspended in the air indefinitely."

Next, she moved on to Silicon's abilities.

"Silicon's powers are my favorite," the guide said with a smile. "Like a liquid cement, Silicon was able to use her Element Blasters to mold and shape durable ceramic objects, shoot ropes and lassos, and even walk on stilts, all made of silicone. She was the true artist of the team."

Brooklyn watched the filmed footage of Silicon in action with a glimmer of childlike joy in her eyes. Steven knew that she was her favorite hero on the team.

The third suit, belonging to Lithium, could shoot electricity out of the Element Blasters, which could power up electronic devices or even short-circuit evil robots. Lithium had even been capable of creating images and shapes in the air with his electricity, like an electrical skywriter.

Beryllium's suit possessed incredibly strong and unbelievably bouncy springs which enabled her to leap a hundred feet into the air. She was also able to fire a spring out of her Element Blaster, which could wrap around or attach to an object and reel it in like a fishing pole.

After exploring a few more exhibits, the tour concluded, and the class explored the rest of the museum on their own for the next hour. After lunch, they headed back outside, where some took selfies in front of the stone fountain. Steven and Brooklyn took one together.

Afterward, Steven gazed at the statues, deep in thought. He wished the Table of Elements were still around. Even though he never met them, Steven felt a strange, personal connection to the team, especially Helium. He couldn't explain it, at least in a way that didn't make him sound looney, but he felt like he had known the hero his whole life. There was something about

Helium that seemed familiar yet … *distant* at the same time. Whatever it was, Steven couldn't put his finger on it.

Steven's deep thoughts were soon broken when the desire came to explore the rest of the outside of the museum. He and Brooklyn walked around the side of the building and were in the middle of observing the giant tree that had caught on fire during the Table of Elements' first outing when Steven discovered a man crossing the street over to the museum.

He was a tall man, with short, spiky brown hair, and a neatly-trimmed brown beard and mustache. He was wearing a pair of blue overalls, thick black boots, Velcro gloves like the kind worn by gardeners and carpenters, and a loose-fitting, red and gray plaid flannel shirt. Due to the spots of dirt on his outfit and the old, worn-out look of his gloves, Steven assumed he had been hard at work.

The man was carrying a cardboard box in front of him that, considering the sweat on his brow and his grunting, seemed too heavy for even someone like him to carry. The box was so large that it covered the front of the man's face. This grew into a real problem quickly, for there was nobody with him, and the man had blindly walked into the street without realizing that there was a massive semi-truck approaching at great speed. Suddenly, the man tripped, and the box fell in front of him.

At once, Steven ran as fast as he could into the middle of the street.

Brooklyn, who had not seen the man or the truck, gasped when she saw Steven suddenly halfway across the street.

"Steven! Look out!" Brooklyn shouted as the truck grew closer.

His heart pounding and his body full of adrenaline, Steven mustered all the strength he had in his five foot seven, 134-pound body and heaved the man out of the way just mere moments before the truck came speeding by, barely missing them by a matter of inches.

"Thank you kindly," said the man as he steadily got to his feet. He had a rich and sophisticated bass voice. It was one of the coolest voices Steven had ever heard, and he hoped that he might have a deep, fancy voice like that when he grew up.

"No problem," said Steven, catching his breath. He was still a little shaken up from the prior event.

Brooklyn finally caught up to him at this time.

"Dude, are you OK?" she asked, her low voice filled with concern.

"Yeah. I-I'm good," said Steven. "Are *you* OK?" he asked the man.

"Yes. Thank you," said the man.

"Here, let us help."

Steven and Brooklyn hoisted up one side of the cardboard box as the man did the other. They navigated their way across the street and set the box down on a little wooden wagon, which seemed to sag under the heaviness of the box.

It was then that Steven and Brooklyn's eyes fell upon the box's contents. It was filled to the brim with old electronic devices, scrap metal, and even what looked like part of an engine, all mixed with random wires, knobs, buttons, and screws.

"Is that a lawn mower engine?" Brooklyn asked, pointing it out.

"Indeed," said the man. "Astounding what you can find around town. To me, these pieces and parts are more precious than diamonds and gold."

"Are you a collector?" Steven assumed.

"Actually," said the man, "I'm an inventor, Mr. …?"

"Starcluster, sir," said Steven, shaking his massive hand. "Steven Starcluster. And this is Brooklyn Adams."

The man's eyes widened.

"*Starcluster,* you say?"

"Yeah. Why?"

The man laughed a little. "It's a very interesting name. And I mean that with good intentions. Would I be correct in assuming that *you're* related to Chief Adams?" he directed at Brooklyn.

"Yes sir," said Brooklyn as she shook his hand, too. "He's my dad."

"Great man, your father," said the man. "Oh, do forgive me. *I* am Reginald Gargon."

"Pleasure to meet you, sir," said Steven pleasantly.

"So … what are you planning to build?" Brooklyn asked.

"I was thinking a robot of some kind," said Mr. Gargon.

"Cool!" said Steven. "I've always wanted a robot. They had some on display in the museum."

Mr. Gargon glanced at the museum behind him.

"*This* one, I take it?"

"Yeah. School field trip," Brooklyn confirmed. "Have you been? It's really something, and I think you'd fit right in with all the techy stuff they've got in there."

"I have yet to visit. Too busy dumpster diving," said Mr. Gargon with a dry chuckle. "But I met the Table of Elements before."

"Really? No way!" said Steven.

"Was it an event or something?" Brooklyn asked.

"Sort of," said Mr. Gargon. "They saved me from a car crash."

Between him and the tour guide, Steven was starting to wonder if there was a single person in San Francisco who *hadn't* been rescued by the Table of Elements.

"They were a truly remarkable group," Mr. Gargon

continued. "I'm pleased to hear they're still looked upon positively even all these years later. If anyone deserves a museum, it's them."

"You wouldn't happen to have known them personally, would you?" Steven asked as soon as the question entered his mind.

"I wish I could say I did," Mr. Gargon answered, "but I had no personal connection to them whatsoever."

"All right," said Steven. "I was just curious. We're huge fans of the team."

"I can see that," said Mr. Gargon, noticing the sweatshirt that Steven was wearing. "I like to think of myself as a fan, too."

"Really?" said Brooklyn, sounding intrigued.

"Yes, indeed. Not to brag, but I consider myself a real Table of Elements expert."

"Does anyone know where Helium is?" Steven asked.

"Not as far as I'm concerned," said Mr. Gargon, looking displeased that he didn't know the answer. "After retiring, Helium never revealed his identity to the public, and honestly, I don't blame him. He deserves a quiet life."

"I agree," said Brooklyn.

"Me too," said Steven. "I like to imagine he's still living in the city as a mild-mannered citizen, going to church, and having a regular job, and all that."

Mr. Gargon smiled before speaking again. "To this day, no one has come around with any news on his whereabouts. I honestly don't think we ever will know where he is."

"That's what I thought," said Brooklyn casually. "Well, it was nice meeting you."

"Likewise," said Mr. Gargon. "Enjoy the rest of your field trip."

Steven and Brooklyn resumed their tree-watching as Mr.

Gargon wheeled his wagon up a path leading north, and he was soon out of sight.

Roughly five minutes later, Mr. Williamson had called everyone back to the bus.

"Thanks for the tour, ma'am," Steven told the tour guide. "It was a blast!"

"You're welcome, young man," said the guide with a cheery smile. "I'm glad you enjoyed it."

Steven and Brooklyn, who had been last in line this time, sat in the front of the bus on the right side. As the vehicle pulled out of the parking lot and onto the street, following Mr. Williamson's car, Steven and Brooklyn discussed the events of their meeting with Mr. Gargon.

"I wonder if he's actually going to build a robot," said Brooklyn.

"Well, he sure had a lot of parts, though I doubt a lawn mower engine's going to be of much use," said Steven.

Then, they turned to the topic of Helium's whereabouts and what Mr. Gargon said on the subject.

"'As far as he's concerned.' " Brooklyn repeated. "So … somebody *might* know where he is."

"Yeah, maybe his family or something," Steven suggested. "You know—people who already knew his secret identity?"

"Do you think he's still in San Francisco?"

"I … really don't know," Steven admitted. "I'd like to think so, but yeah … I agree with Mr. Gargon. I don't think we'll ever know where he is, and I think that's OK."

"Totally," said Brooklyn. "He should be able to live a quiet life without people bothering him."

Steven wished *he* could do the same when he saw Eddie get up from his seat in the back and approach him and Brooklyn.

Why did he have to come over? Steven scrunched up his face at the thought. What was he going to do now?

"I can't believe you went out of your way to talk to a tour guide, Starcluster!" said Eddie. "Oh, wait … I can! Because you're *weird!*"

Steven thought that insult was pretty pathetic. It seemed like Eddie was just forcing himself to find things to mock Steven about, to be as annoying as possible. Steven stayed quiet, staring straight ahead.

"I think you should sit back down, Eddie," said Brooklyn.

"Aww," said Eddie in a baby voice. "Steven's wittle girlfwiend is defending him! Wow, Starcluster! What's wrong? Too chicken to tell me yourself?"

Steven clenched his fists so tightly that his nails dug into his palms. He prayed to stay calm but could feel himself growing more enraged by the moment.

"Leave him alone," said Brooklyn through gritted teeth.

"Or what?" snapped Eddie. "Your dad will arrest me? That loser couldn't catch a crook if one ran right by him!"

Steven had finally had it. He had known Chief Adams for four years. The Chief occasionally gave him and Brooklyn rides home from school and taught him about several police things. He was an amazing police officer and, above all, a brave and honorable Christian man. He wasn't going to let anyone insult Brooklyn's father.

"Be quiet!" Steven roared. He stood up at once and glared at Eddie, feeling angrier than ever.

"Make me!" yelled Eddie.

Steven screamed at the top of his lungs as he mustered up all his strength and shoved Eddie as hard as possible.

*   *   *

An hour and a half later, Steven told his dad at the hospital about what happened on the bus that caused it to crash. His eyes watered like a faucet, and his voice stuttered with sadness as he said, "I pushed Eddie. Brooklyn and I were s-s-sitting near the front row, and s-s-so Eddie crashed into the bus driver, which ... caused him to lose control and accidentally drive off the road ... The Presidio Parkway. I was scared ... the b-b-bus drove off the bridge and flipped over!"

Steven began to cry just as soon as he finished telling his dad.

Boaz didn't move a muscle. He was shocked to the core. Steven, his wonderful son whom he loved with all his heart— the same kid always praised by the neighbors, parents, and teachers for his kindness, manners, and polite attitude—had caused the terrible accident that hurt everyone on the bus.

"I'm glad you're OK," Boaz said softly. "But I'm still very disappointed in you."

Boaz's voice became firmer, and he did not smile.

"Why did you push him? It's not like you to act that way."

Steven was having a difficult time looking his dad in the eyes.

"Eddie had been picking on me all day. And he insulted Brooklyn's dad, too. He called him a loser! I should have known better than to shove him, but I couldn't help it! He's been bullying me since sixth grade. I've bottled up my anger every day for the past four years. I felt like I was going to explode! I lost my temper and now ... everyone h-has to suffer for it! I'm sorry, Dad! I'm so sorry!"

"It's OK," said Boaz calmly. "I'm not mad. The doctor told me they would run more tests tomorrow; then, you can come home. Thankfully, you and Brooklyn don't have any broken bones, unlike ..."

Boaz stopped himself, but it was too late. Steven had already picked up on what he'd almost said. Some kids had broken bones.

"*I* did that to them!" Steven cried.

"It's all right!" Boaz pleaded. "Please, keep your voice down."

"No one's ever going to talk to me again because of this!"

"Shhhhhhhhh," said Boaz comfortingly as he fluffed Steven's pillow. "You are a terrific kid. You're smart, kind, and respectful, and I love you. Now please, get some sleep. I promise that it will be all right. Take a deep breath, rest your eyes, and think happy thoughts. It will be OK."

Boaz's calming voice soothed his son like a steaming towel to the face. Steven gently rested his head on his pillow and sighed.

"If the Table of Elements were still here, maybe they could have saved us from the crash," he said.

Boaz said nothing for a while. He closed his eyes sorrowfully. Eventually, with his calm tone unchanged, he said, "Get some rest. Doctor's orders."

Steven started to speak again. "But what about everyone else?"

"Just relax," Boaz ordered softly. "They'll be all right."

"I'm so sorry," said Steven.

"I know you are," said Boaz.

He sat in a chair by the window and rested his cane beside it.

"I'll stay with you until you're able to come home. Just promise me you'll go to sleep."

*   *   *

Steven couldn't remember the last time he slept so poorly. All night, he experienced dreadful nightmares from what he'd caused on the school bus. The horror and pain on everyone's face made it nearly impossible not to cry, even in a dream.

Finally, he awoke in the early morning hours with a sharp jolt, frightened and gasping for breath. The curtains to the window were opened, showing the city lit up by beautiful lights, which could still be seen through heavy rain and thunder.

It took a few seconds for Steven to realize that he was back in reality, but the images of his nightmares still flashed before his eyes. He turned to the clock hanging on the wall above the door.

Three AM.

Steven desperately wanted time to stop where it was. He knew that everyone would be angry with him when he returned to school. If he was unpopular with the students before, Steven felt that it was nothing compared to how much more he would be now.

Steven looked around the room. Boaz was fast asleep on top of the covers of the second bed. As much as Steven wanted to talk to him, he refused because he thought it would be impolite to wake his father. He sighed. It was nights like these when he wished he had his mother with him.

Steven's mother was Andrea Starcluster, who sadly passed away when he was only a toddler. For reasons unknown, Boaz rarely spoke about his mother. Steven assumed it was because he was still heartbroken by the loss of his wife, but Steven often thought there was more to it if only he knew. He hardly remembered his mother since he was so young when she passed away, but he did remember her always talking about God and reading him Bible stories before bed. He was happy to say that both his parents were strong Christians who taught him to love and obey the Lord.

Suddenly, Steven smiled a little. He realized he didn't need to talk to his mother *or* father at that moment. He already had someone to talk to—someone whom he could talk to for as long as he wanted—someone who would help him entirely. Gently, Steven closed his eyes, folded his hands, and bowed his head.

"Lord Jesus," he prayed, "I'm praying to You right now because I'm overwhelmed with guilt. People from my school are in the hospital because I got angry and took it out on another person. I'm so sorry for what I did. Please forgive me for the sins I've committed. Please take this wickedness away from me and give me the strength to control my anger and be loving toward others. And thank You that Brooklyn and I are all right. I love You and I worship You. In Jesus's Name, I pray, Amen."

Steven took a deep breath upon closing in prayer. He knew he had asked for forgiveness and was truly remorseful for his actions, but he didn't feel forgiven. Guilt was still flowing through him like a disease, and he felt like he could only be cured if he paid off his debt by making it up to God and his schoolmates. He was never going to make another mistake like the one he made on the school bus—never again.

CHAPTER THREE

T HE DOCTORS RAN more tests on Steven and Brooklyn in the morning. After finding them to be perfectly fine, they were permitted to go home with Boaz and Chief Adams respectively.

"I'm glad you're OK," Brooklyn told Steven in the lobby. "I don't know what I'd do without you."

"Me neither," Steven agreed. "You mean the world to me."

Steven feared that he would be suspended from school because of his actions and expressed these concerns to his father. But he and Boaz talked with Principal Sanchez later that same day, who informed them that Steven would not be suspended, considering the school's "three-strike" policy. She told Steven and Boaz that this was Steven's first strike, and two more would mean a week-long suspension.

After the meeting with the principal, Steven and Boaz met with Brooklyn's father at the San Francisco Police Department. In his office, Chief Adams questioned Steven about the cause of the wreck. He let Steven off the hook when he heard his and Boaz's side of the story, but not without a final notice.

"I've known you for years, Steven. You're a good kid, and you have a big heart. But don't think that just because you're my daughter's best friend, I'm going to let you off without a warning. Stay out of trouble and control your anger. You won't get off so easy next time. I'm sorry, but that's how it is."

"Thank you, sir," said Steven, shaking his hand.

After the meeting, Steven and Boaz left the Chief's office and returned to their parked car. Steven still felt guilty for the accident he'd caused, but at the same time, he felt relieved that he wasn't fined, sentenced to a court date, or even suspended from school.

Steven shared his feelings with Boaz as they climbed into the car and buckled their seatbelts.

"That went better than I thought," he said. "I can't believe I'm not getting punished!"

"Oh no, you'll still have a punishment," Boaz replied as he turned on the car and pulled out of the parking spot.

"Wait, what?" Steven asked, laughing in disbelief. He wasn't sure if this was one of his dad's jokes or if he was being legitimately serious.

"I know you're sorry," said Boaz. He didn't sound at all angry or stern. "But you still did something wrong. Therefore, you will still have a punishment."

Boaz grounded Steven from watching TV for a week and gave him some extra chores to do around the house for the rest of the day. Steven wasn't happy about not being able to watch

TV, but he knew that Boaz only punished him because he loved him, and Steven didn't complain once.

Since he couldn't watch TV, he entertained himself after completing his chores by admiring the view of Union Square from the sitting room window. He had more fun than he thought he'd have as he watched the cars driving by and the ant-sized people hurrying from one place to another. Steven liked to imagine what interesting errands or adventures were going on, even if they were highly imaginative and unrealistic. Best of all, he liked to joke, there were no ads or commercials.

FRIDAY, MARCH 12TH

"I'm trying to look at the bright side of it," Steven told Brooklyn as they rode down their building's elevator. "At least I get to spend time with a great view. TV's not the most important thing anyway."

"Yeah," said Brooklyn, "but the new episode of *Zeke the Funniest* airs today after school."

Steven's heart sank because *Zeke the Funniest* was his all-time favorite show. He felt a little disappointed that he couldn't watch the new episode that day, or the next *six* days for that matter, but didn't show it because he was trying to behave perfectly.

"Bye, Dad," said Steven as he and Brooklyn passed Boaz's office in the lobby.

"See you later, Boaz," said Brooklyn.

Both Boaz and Brooklyn's father were OK with her calling him by his first name since Boaz and her dad were very close friends, just like Steven and Brooklyn.

"Bye, kids." Boaz waved back at them, smiling pleasantly. "Have a good day at school."

Steven and Brooklyn left the building, turned left, and headed up Stockton Street. San Francisco was partly cloudy that day, and the temperature was cool as usual.

"At least the episode's free to stream," said Steven, returning to the prior conversation. "Oh, what do you know? A dime."

He picked the small silver coin up off the sidewalk and slipped it into his jeans pocket.

"Eh," he continued in a bored tone as he shrugged. "You can't really buy anything with it anyway."

"Well, you can donate it to charity or put it in your bank," Brooklyn pointed out.

Steven laughed. "That would just be sad! The bankers would say sarcastic stuff like, 'Oh! You certainly worked hard today, eh young man?'"

Brooklyn laughed with him. After some seconds, their minds refocused on school and their classmates from the accident.

"Do you think everyone's all right?" Steven asked nervously.

"I hope so," said Brooklyn, her tone similar to his. "It's been almost two days after all."

"I couldn't live with myself if I caused someone's death," said Steven miserably.

"It was an accident, dude," said Brooklyn. "If *we* recovered this quickly, why shouldn't everyone else?"

"I … I don't know," said Steven, his mental state unchanged.

They turned left on Pine Street. Steven's melancholy expression froze as he stared at their school.

"Don't worry, dude," said Brooklyn. "It's not going to be that bad. You made a mistake, but that's all in the past. And no matter what happens, I'll be by your side."

Brooklyn kindly placed her hand on Steven's shoulder. Steven turned around and smiled at her.

"You're right, Brooklyn," he agreed. "I'm being too hard on myself. It's probably not going to be that bad."

With those words, Steven straightened his back and marched up to the school with Brooklyn beside him. Steven arrived at the entrance first. Then, reminding himself to be on his best behavior, he held one of the glass doors open for Brooklyn.

"Thanks," she said as she passed him.

Steven smiled. It felt good to be thanked. He entered the building after Brooklyn and closed the door behind him. Brooklyn froze in place, just like Steven had earlier.

"What's wrong?" Steven asked. Then, he gazed down the hall and realized why Brooklyn had halted. Over thirty students stood by their lockers with the angriest faces Steven had ever seen. What made it worse was the fact that all these furious faces were aimed directly at *him*. Most of the kids were sophomores from the school bus incident (Steven could tell because of their casts and bandages), and the others probably had been informed about the crash by the victims.

Everyone stood in their places and said nothing.

Finally, after what seemed like an hour, Steven reluctantly smiled and attempted to lighten the mood.

"Hey, guys. We're all together again, eh?" he said, chuckling weakly.

Everyone was silent, as though time had stopped.

"That hospital food was pretty good, right?" Steven continued. "I mean, their pancakes were the fifteenth greatest ones I've ever had. Yes, I-I keep records."

Still, no one spoke.

"It's … uh … nice to see all your happy faces," Steven said cautiously.

That made everyone glare even more.

"Are you guys still angry at me?" Steven asked without taking a breath.

"I think we should get to class, dude," said Brooklyn.

She grabbed Steven by the wrist and walked him down the hall before he could say anything else. Steven covered his face in embarrassment, wishing he had stayed quiet.

They soon made it to their homeroom and met their teacher by the door.

"Oh!" she exclaimed, appearing taken aback at the sight of Steven. "Hello—ahem!—Hello … Steven."

By the look on her face, Steven could tell that she also knew what he had done.

"Hello, Mrs. Allison," Steven responded, struggling to look at her directly.

Steven and Brooklyn found their desks and sat down. The class didn't start for a few more minutes, so they talked to pass the time.

"Yessiree. People are still angry at me." Steven slumped at his desk, resting his head on his hand.

"Well, at least they aren't avoiding you," Brooklyn chimed in positively.

"I think it would've been better if they did," Steven returned. "Seeing everyone glaring at me is a lot worse, in my opinion."

"Don't let it get to you, dude," said Brooklyn. "I'd guess the Table of Elements made the bad guys angry by putting them in jail. People even got angry at Jesus and the apostles."

"Yeah, but they were disliked even though they did *good* things. I did something *bad*. I doubt I'd have been a good apostle, and I doubt the Table of Elements would've allowed me on their team, either. It breaks my heart knowing that the heroes of San Francisco—*my* heroes—would turn me down like a clump of dirt."

Before Brooklyn could respond, the other students entered the room and took their seats just before the bell rang. Homeroom had begun, and Steven and Brooklyn would have to wait an hour before they could talk again.

*   *   *

At noon, the students were excused for lunch. Whereas most ate cafeteria food, Steven and Brooklyn ate bagged lunches from home. The two of them sat at a table in the center of the cafeteria, their minds off the subject of the school bus incident.

"What kind of sandwich you got?" asked Brooklyn.

"Peanut butter and jelly today," Steven answered, inspecting the contents of his lunch bag. "I like that my dad remembers I try to keep things simple."

"That explains why your favorite color is gray," Brooklyn pointed out.

"Well—wait … 'gray?'"

"Yeah," said Brooklyn.

Steven laughed. "My favorite color's *blue!* Royal blue!"

Brooklyn looked shocked. Steven wasn't sure if she was going to start laughing or not.

"You're kidding!" she said.

"I'm shocked *you* weren't!" said Steven. "I would have thought you'd know your best friend's favorite color."

Suddenly, Brooklyn's smile dropped.

"What?" Steven asked.

Brooklyn motioned to the doors with her head. Steven turned around and stared in that direction. His heart skipped a beat, and he almost dropped his sandwich. Two tall, muscular boys, on either side of a sophomore in a wheelchair, were walking toward them with faces that meant trouble. The two standing up had not been on the school bus the day of the wreck but acted as henchmen to someone who *had* been. The one in the wheelchair was their leader, Eddie Macaron, with his leg in a cast.

"Hey, Starcluster!" Eddie snapped as he and his goons arrived at the table.

"Hey, Eddie," said Steven nervously. "How are you?"

It felt strange for Steven that the wheelchair made Eddie the same height as him, and he was struggling to stay calm.

"Well, I have been doing rather fine," Eddie said carelessly as he looked up at the ceiling thoughtfully. Then, he shot a mean look at Steven and continued in a much tougher voice, "If you leave out the part about me *breaking my leg,* all because of *you!*"

"I didn't mean to get you put in the hospital!" Steven explained. "I'm sorry."

"That apology is not going to heal my leg, Starcluster!" Eddie barked.

"Leave him alone, Eddie," Brooklyn ordered.

"I don't take orders from anyone, Adams! I'm here to make sure your friend gets what he deserves."

"Hold on!" Brooklyn pleaded. "We don't have to resort to violence. Is there anything we can do to help you?"

"No," said Eddie with a glare.

"D-do you want me to sign your cast?" Steven asked, hoping for a positive response. "I ... I can write in cursive!"

"No!" Eddie growled.

"Bubble letters?"

"No! I don't want anyone to sign my cast!" Eddie roared. "I'm here to give you a little 'signature' of my own."

Eddie turned to his henchmen.

"Guys?"

One of them stepped forward and drew back his fist as quickly as he could. Poor Steven didn't have time to protect himself. The boy's fist flew back down like a rock as he punched Steven right in the face.

CHAPTER FOUR

B OAZ RETURNED TO his apartment at noon for lunch. It was a nice simple lunch—a lettuce and turkey sandwich with an apple, which he ate at the kitchen counter.

As he ate, Boaz noticed the old photo album collection under the sitting room's coffee table. After he finished his lunch, he washed his dishes and limped over to the sitting room on his cane, thinking it would be nice to crack open those books and reminisce on fun family memories.

He pulled out the large red one, the first one on the shelf, and opened it on his lap as he sat in the forest-green armchair behind the coffee table. It had been over a year since he had looked at any of these albums. This one in particular he hadn't viewed in a few years at least. Boaz was sure that Steven was still in middle school the last time he'd opened it.

He immediately recognized some of the photos—Steven's

first trip to the dentist, Steven's first baseball game, and Steven's first day of school. He chuckled when he saw Steven grinning ear-to-ear at Pier 39 after getting a lollipop that was almost the size of his head. The sugar rush kept him up nearly all night.

After admiring those photos, Boaz closed the album and opened a blue one. This was one of the oldest ones he had. It was also the one that pained him to look through the most. This album contained photos from his college days. He immediately recognized his best friends, Robert and Charlotte, and his wife-to-be, Andrea, who had the most beautiful smile he had ever seen.

Boaz turned toward the end of the book where his wedding photos were. Robert stood beside him, and Charlotte stood beside Andrea. Everyone looked so happy. Boaz bowed his head sorrowfully after seeing a photo of him and Andrea eating their wedding cake.

The image that nearly made him shed a tear was taken several years after graduating college. It showed him, Robert, and a third man standing together, smiling, under a shady tree in Golden Gate Park. This third man was tall, broad-shouldered, and muscular, with blond hair and a thin mustache. Boaz remembered his name like it was an annoying song stuck in his head: Tyler Tarsus. The sight of Tarsus dismayed him to his core. They had been good friends, but that was in the past. Tarsus had been responsible for something terrible. Something—

Boaz was suddenly interrupted by his ringing cell phone, which he had left on the kitchen counter. He closed the photo album and hobbled to the counter to answer it.

"Hello?" he said.

"Mr. Starcluster?" said a voice he recognized as the voice of Principal Sanchez.

"Speaking."

"Your son is hurt," said the principal.

Boaz froze. " 'Hurt?' " he repeated.

"A student gave him a black eye and shoved him to the floor. He's in the nurse's office as we speak."

At once Boaz drove to the school, picked up his son, and helped him inside the penthouse. Steven was clutching his face while moaning in pain.

"Easy," said Boaz calmly. "Let's sit you down."

Boaz walked his son past the kitchen and into the dining room, where he pulled out a wooden chair and sat Steven at the table.

"Let me see your eye," said Boaz.

Carefully, Steven raised the dripping bag of ice off his face.

"Oh!" Boaz gasped.

"How … how does it look?" Steven asked hesitantly.

"It's black and swollen."

"Great," said Steven miserably, rolling his good eye. "I have a prune in my socket."

"I'll get you another icepack."

Boaz headed to the freezer. "What happened this time?" he asked from the kitchen.

Steven spoke weakly as though he had just woken up from a scary dream. He told Boaz about the lunch incident and how Eddie was angry with him and had one of his friends punch him in the face.

"The punch was so hard that I nearly blacked out," Steven continued as Boaz returned with a new icepack for him. "Eddie got detention, and I got taken to the nurse's office. This was the last day before Spring Break. So, they said it wasn't a big deal if I went home early."

Boaz handed the icepack to Steven, who pressed it against his eye.

"Thanks for picking me up."

"Of course," said Boaz. "I'm just glad you're not seriously hurt."

"I am, Dad," Steven said quietly.

"I'm sorry?" asked Boaz, who hadn't heard him properly.

"I *am* seriously hurt," Steven repeated in a clearer voice.

Boaz sighed in a way that let Steven know that he understood and cared. "I get it," he said. "It's a terrible experience being beaten up by a bully."

"It's not that," said Steven, not sounding rude at all. "It's just that I now know the truth—I'm not forgiven. I made one gigantic mistake, and the entire school hates me for it!"

"Steven!" Boaz said comfortingly.

Immediately, Steven stood up. His body shook like a leaf in Autumn. "I know these people, and they didn't care for me *before* the bus incident! I'm stuck with this mistake for the rest of my life!"

Though it must have hurt his head, Steven rocketed out of the dining room and up the stairs, his eyes swimming in tears.

*   *   *

It took a lot of work for Brooklyn to concentrate on school the rest of the day. Thinking of Steven alone at home with a black eye made it difficult for her to focus during Chemistry. When the bell rang at three o'clock that afternoon, Brooklyn hurried to her locker and grabbed her things. She wanted to head over to Steven's immediately to check on him.

As she opened her locker, a teacher with glasses and a brown bob cut approached her. It was Mrs. Hildebrandt, Brooklyn's math teacher.

"Hello, Brooklyn," she said.

"Hi, Mrs. Hildebrandt," said Brooklyn.

"How's Steven doing?"

"I'm not sure," said Brooklyn. "He's at home right now. I was going to go see him."

"Well, I hope he's feeling better," said Mrs. Hildebrandt. "What happened in the cafeteria was appalling, regardless of what happened on the bus. When will people learn that two wrongs don't make a right?"

Brooklyn was happy to hear that Mrs. Hildebrandt was concerned about Steven's well-being. A part of her had assumed that she was going to criticize him instead. She was glad that her assumption had been wrong.

"Well, I should probably get going," said Brooklyn. She grabbed her backpack from her locker, but she accidentally grabbed it by the wrong end, causing most of the contents to spill out.

"Here, let me help," said Mrs. Hildebrandt kindly.

The two of them gathered all the supplies from the backpack and put them back inside as neatly as before. Mrs. Hildebrandt's eyes fell on one of the last things still on the floor: Brooklyn's notebook, which was opened to one of the middle pages. To Brooklyn's horror, Mrs. Hildebrandt noticed her drawing on the page. It was a large heart with a detailed outline. In the middle, it had two names connected by a plus sign—Steven and Brooklyn.

Brooklyn blushed, which was something she seldom did. She quickly grabbed the notebook, closed it, and returned it to her backpack.

"Sorry," said Mrs. Hildebrandt. "I didn't mean to peek. It was just … open right there …"

"It's fine," said Brooklyn quickly as she grabbed her skateboard and closed her locker. "Have a … have a good break."

"You, too," said Mrs. Hildebrandt.

As far as Brooklyn was concerned, Mrs. Hildebrandt was the first to discover that she had a secret crush on Steven, and it was a huge fear for her that Steven might find out. Well, maybe not "fear," but "concern" at least. Steven was the funniest, nicest guy she knew, but he was also her best friend. They had known each other since the sixth grade, and Brooklyn didn't know how it would affect their friendship if she told him how she felt. What if Steven didn't like her back, and things became awkward? Brooklyn hoped she would have the courage to finally tell him one day before it was too late. She feared the thought of Steven going to prom in the future with a gorgeous girlfriend while Brooklyn stood in the shadows by the bleachers. For now, she was just Steven's friend, and for the most part, she was fine with that.

With Steven still on her mind, Brooklyn left Pine Tree High, pulled out her phone, and called his number. He didn't pick up. Disappointed, she called his father's number instead, and to her delight, she got an answer this time.

"Hi, Boaz," she said. "I was wondering if it would be OK if I came over to see Steven?"

"Certainly," said Boaz cheerfully over the phone. "Your father's here, too."

"Steven didn't commit a crime, did he?" Brooklyn joked.

"No, your dad and I are just chatting," Boaz replied. "We've been discussing some … important things … and we think it's best to tell you and Steven about them in person."

Important things about her and Steven? Were they referring to college plans? Or was it a surprise trip for Spring Break? The latter seemed more likely. Brooklyn just hoped it was good news.

"I'll be right over," she said.

Brooklyn skateboarded down to Union Square, then stopped in front of BRCA Apartments. She took the elevator to the top floor and knocked on Boaz's door. She was let inside by Boaz himself and could see her dad sitting on the couch in the sitting room.

"Hey, Dad," she greeted, high-fiving him.

"How was school?" asked the Chief.

"Not the best," Brooklyn admitted. "Don't know if Boaz told you, but Steven got beat up at lunch. It was horrible. How is he now?" she asked Boaz.

"He's still pretty bent out of shape," said Boaz. "He feels very guilty for what happened on the bus. I've never seen him this worked up before."

"Brooklyn and I have been praying for him," said Chief Adams. "Steven's a good kid."

"I appreciate that, Andrew," said Boaz.

"Is there anything we can do to cheer him up?" Brooklyn asked.

A grin slowly stretched across Boaz's face. He looked at Chief Adams.

"That's what your dad and I wanted to talk to the two of you about," Boaz answered.

"We've considered it for a while," added the Chief, "but didn't think it was right. Now, we think you're ready to know."

"Know what?" asked Brooklyn. Boaz and her dad were acting very mysterious. Why were they smiling like that?

"My involvement …" Boaz started slowly, "with the *Table of Elements.*"

Brooklyn stood in silence. "You don't mean—"

Boaz and Chief Adams nodded.

Brooklyn gasped. "No way!" she said in a hushed voice. Her mouth hung open like a goldfish at a surprise party and her eyes nearly burst out of her head.

CHAPTER FIVE

THE BLINDS WERE closed upstairs as Steven lay on the couch in the TV room with his face buried deep into a pillow.

"Father," he prayed, "I'm sorry that I'm not perfect. Please help me to do what's right in Your eyes. I can't bear to make another mistake again! I pray that You will allow something to happen that will help me clear my name. In Jesus's name, I pray. Amen."

After he finished his prayer, he rested again. Flashbacks of the school bus crash and the incident in the cafeteria ran through his mind in a continuous loop. He scrunched up his face in anguish as he relived those traumatizing moments. Would the guilt and pain ever go away? He wasn't sure.

It was then that he heard a familiar voice across the room. "Hey, dude."

Steven didn't need to look up to know who that was. He sat up slowly.

"Hey, Brooklyn," he said calmly.

Despite the depression he was going through, Steven was happy to see her. After all, she was his best friend—his gal pal—and he loved her with all his heart.

Brooklyn sat at the other end of the couch after Steven moved his legs out of the way.

"How are you feeling?" she asked.

"I'm a little better now," Steven confessed, "but I'm far from happy. How was the rest of school?"

"It was hard to focus," said Brooklyn. "I kept thinking about you."

She paused. "I'm sorry about what happened, dude. But I want you to know that I was never mad at you for what happened on the bus. Neither was my dad. Even Mrs. Hildebrandt asked how you were."

"Really?"

"Yeah, she thought it was awful what Eddie and his friends did to you," said Brooklyn. "Regardless of what happened on the bus, I'm still by your side. You're still my best friend, and, more importantly, God loves you."

Steven smiled weakly. "Thanks, Brooklyn. I don't know what I'd do without a friend like you."

He and Brooklyn hugged, but deep down, Steven still felt guilty.

"Now, if you're feeling better, Boaz and my dad have a little surprise for us," Brooklyn announced. "I think it will cheer you up."

Steven sighed. "All right," he said, "but I don't know what could possibly cheer me up right now. Unless it can make everyone forget about my ... mistake."

Brooklyn grinned. "Trust me, dude. You will be surprised," she said, enunciating the last four words.

Brooklyn led Steven downstairs to the dining room table. Boaz and Chief Adams were already there. Steven expected to see them discussing work or reading the news or something. But instead, the two men were thumb-wrestling to pass the time. Brooklyn gave a brief laugh at the sight. Even Steven had to admit that it was pretty funny. As soon as he and Brooklyn arrived at the table, Boaz and Chief Adams stopped what they were doing and gave them their full attention.

"How are you feeling, Steven?" Boaz asked.

"Fine," said Steven, forcing back a laugh. "Thumb wrestling, huh?"

"What's wrong with it?" said Boaz with a sly grin.

"I don't know," said Steven.

"Just not the manliest thing, I guess," Brooklyn added.

"I'm sorry; you wanted us to start chopping firewood and fixing cars in the sixty-five seconds you left us?" Chief Adams joked with them.

"Sixty-*seven* seconds actually," said Brooklyn with a smug look.

Chief Adams immediately dropped his eyebrows so that they formed almost a straight line. He held his index finger and thumb so close together that one might think he was holding an ant between them.

"You're *this* close to being arrested for mocking the chief of police, young lady," he said with a twinkle in his eye.

Boaz chuckled. "Have a seat," he said as he motioned to the chairs on the other side of the table.

Steven and Brooklyn took their seats as instructed.

"So … what's going on?" Steven asked politely as he folded his hands on top of the table.

"Your dad's going to talk about the Table of Elements," Brooklyn told him.

"Really?" Steven said in surprise. "Wow! I'm ... I'm ... w-what exactly do you want to say about them?"

Steven glanced over at Brooklyn, and confusion coursed through his brain. She looked like she was forcing back the most exciting news in the world. Steven wondered if he looked as ecstatic as she did the day of the field trip.

"We'd tell you, but I think Brooklyn will explode if *she* doesn't get to do it," Chief Adams answered.

An enormous expression of relief appeared on Brooklyn's face. At once, she spun around, which wasn't the easiest thing to do in a wooden chair, and exclaimed in a very fast voice, "Boaz was a member of the Table of Elements!"

"Really? That's cool. So what did you—" Steven froze mid-sentence. "Wait, *what?*" he cried. His mouth hung open wide. "You're ... you're serious?"

Brooklyn nodded, looking much more casual this time.

Steven swung his head back to Boaz and Chief Adams. "You ... you were ... you were ... *Table of Elements?*" Steven was practically wheezing. He didn't know what to say. Boaz was fun, brave, and cool, but could he really have been a member of the Table of Elements? *The* Table of Elements?

At this point, Steven remembered how much Boaz and Brooklyn liked to joke around with him. His face relaxed at this thought, and he smiled at his dad in a "You got me" kind of way. "All right, all right," he said, chuckling. "Good one. Very funny."

Steven might have smiled, but he was a little disappointed that it had been nothing more than an elaborate prank. Still, he fell for it, so he had to admit it had been good.

"It's not a joke, Steven," said Boaz. He didn't smile. There wasn't a single trace of silliness in his voice or eyes.

Steven froze again. Once more, his smile vanished like an extinguished candle. "You're serious," he said aloud. It was a realization, not a question.

Boaz and Chief Adams both nodded professionally.

"Woah," said Steven.

"Woah, indeed!" Brooklyn added.

"This is … this is *cool!*" Steven continued. He was so stunned that he could think of no other word to describe it. "The two of you were superheroes?"

"*I* wasn't," Chief Adams confirmed. "Just Boaz."

Steven had a million questions running through his head. They were overwhelming him. He could tell that Brooklyn was feeling the same way. She spoke up before he could. However, her two questions had been just what *he* had wanted to ask.

"How did you become a member? What's your origin?"

Boaz cleared his throat. "In my first year of college, I met the woman who would soon be my wife, Andrea, and future Table of Elements members, Robert and Charlotte, who would become Lithium and Beryllium. We quickly became best friends and hung out together all the time. I would not even be a Christian today if it weren't for their example.

"We were always in the same classes at Golden Gate U. All of us majored in engineering and minored in chemistry. It was during our time in college when we realized that we could combine our two subjects and use our knowledge of them to make something wonderful. When we were twenty-one years old, we put our engineering skills to the task and designed our Table of Elements armor and Element Blasters while employed at the university's lab."

Steven listened to every word Boaz said. He savored each

syllable like he was eating a filet mignon. He had dreamed of hearing this story for as long as he could remember.

"I was Helium," Boaz continued, "Robert was Lithium, Charlotte was Beryllium, and Andrea was Silicon. Together, the four of us became the Table of Elements, the heroes of San Francisco."

"No way!" Steven's eyes and smile grew. "We're the first people to ever hear the true origin story of San Francisco's greatest superheroes!"

"*Only* superheroes, dude," Brooklyn corrected.

"What about the mascot for that cheeseburger place? The one with the cape. Doesn't he count?" Steven asked.

Brooklyn pondered for a moment, then shrugged. "OK, you got me there. Anyone who can cook a burger as good as that is a superhero to me."

"We got permission from the mayor to use our inventions to protect the people of San Francisco, and the city's police chief deputized us," Boaz continued. "We promised never to take a life no matter the circumstance and agreed to never harm a human being unless in self-defense. We were successful with our work and kept the city safe during the nine years we were operational. Then, thirteen years ago, we held a team meeting on a space station ... with an ... ally ... of ours named ... named ... Tyler Tarsus."

He paused. He looked depressed. "We met him a few years before ... before ..."

Boaz's voice trailed off as his eyes glued themselves to the table. "He seemed very different than the façade he wore," he soon continued. "I knew him when I was a kid back in elementary school. He was my best friend. He moved away at the end of our fourth-grade year, and I didn't see him again until we were adults. I was happy to have my old friend back.

He became friends with Andrea, Robert, and Charlotte, too. We started having fun together as a group of five. He gained our trust … and our friendship. He was resourceful and clever. After much consideration, we trained him to be a Table of Elements member. Then … then … we invited him to the space station we used as a backup base to officially make him part of the team."

Boaz stopped again before continuing in a much more solemn voice. "That was the day the Table of Elements … were *finished*."

*   *   *

Thirteen Years Ago

Despite the cold, dark environment of the Srilvakor Solar System surrounding them, the space station felt warm and comfortable. The Table of Elements had always been a group of four—the four musketeers—and now they were opening their welcoming arms even further to allow a fifth companion to join their party.

Boaz, Andrea, Robert, and Charlotte stood around a wide, round table in the middle of the command room of the station. Boaz and Robert were wearing their best suits (normal ones, not super-suits) and Andrea and Charlotte wore beautiful suit dresses. Andrea even wore her hair up in a French twist.

On the other side of the table stood Tyler Tarsus, his blond hair as tidy as usual. His professional smile seemed to be suppressing the unbridled joy he was feeling, and Boaz wasn't surprised in the slightest. It was a dream come true for his friend, and he was delighted to have Tyler in the ranks.

The Table of Elements gently placed the front of their

hands on individual panels on top of the table. A light inside scanned their hands before a couple of beeps and a sharp click emanated from the surface. There was a hissing of air as a small platform ascended from an opened table compartment. On top of the platform was a small glass box, which opened on its own as soon as it reached eye level. The box contained a brand-new pair of Element Blasters, made just for Tyler, who eyed them like a kid in a toy store.

Robert was the first to speak. "Tyler Tarsus, in the three years we've known you, you have proven yourself to be brave, resourceful, and above all, loyal."

"We are proud and honored to accept you as the newest edition to our team," Andrea continued. "And it's an even bigger honor to present to you these brand-new titanium Element Blasters."

"We trust that you will use these for good," Charlotte joined in. "To help the people of San Francisco."

"We're proud of you, Tyler," Boaz concluded. "You've been a good friend, and we're sure you'll make a wonderful hero. Welcome to the Table of Elements."

The four heroes applauded their new recruit, who bowed in a very theatrical manner.

"Thank you, thank you!" said Tyler. "I'm honored to be a part of this astonishing group."

The next few minutes were spent diving into the amazing cake and punch that the group had prepared for the occasion. The five of them laughed and talked as they snacked on the party treats. Then, when Boaz went into the kitchen to grab a refill, Andrea tagged along, leaving Robert and Charlotte with Tyler.

Boaz hummed pleasantly as he poured himself some punch.

"Top you off?" he asked his wife with a cool grin as he held up an empty cup.

"Most obliged, sir," said Andrea, playing along.

Boaz poured another drink and handed it to his wife.

He and Andrea clinked their paper cups together, even though it was impossible to make such a sound with the material. They didn't mind though. It was the thought that counted.

"You know, our anniversary's tomorrow," Boaz reminded.

"Really?" said Andrea with a smile forming at the corner of her mouth.

"I wanted to wait until then to give you this, but I figured you can't find a more special space … than *space!*"

He chuckled a little sheepishly. It was a pretty mediocre joke, but Andrea didn't seem to mind.

Boaz pulled a small golden box out of his suit pocket and presented it to her. Andrea carefully pulled back the ribbon and opened the box like it was on a hinge. She gasped softly. Lying on a velvet cushion was a golden bracelet, which shimmered in the fluorescent light above.

"There's more," said Boaz calmly. "Open it."

Andrea did this. The locket on the bracelet had a black and white photo of her, Boaz, and baby Steven inside. It was taken in front of the Palace of Fine Arts in San Francisco on a sunny spring day. It was Andrea's favorite photo of them, and the look of awe and gratitude on her face assured Boaz that it still was.

"Boaz, it's beautiful!" said Andrea, clutching the present to her chest.

"Happy anniversary, honey," said Boaz.

Andrea smiled at her husband, holding the bracelet in her hand. Boaz smiled back. The two leaned in and kissed tenderly. With Tyler now installed and a wonderful anniversary dinner to look forward to tomorrow, everything seemed as chipper as a day in the sun.

Then the rain began to pour.

Boaz and Andrea broke apart. They heard yelling from the other room. At first, Boaz assumed that Tyler and the others were just horsing around, but then, to his and Andrea's unexpected shock, they heard a powerful *BANG!* A massive cube-shaped dent appeared in the heavy metal door.

Boaz's body turned to ice. That door was four inches thick. The only thing strong enough on the station to possibly make a dent that size and that deep was the titanium from …

Oh no.

Boaz clicked the open button on the control panel, but the deep dent prevented the door from fully retracting. Boaz and Andrea slid under the door at exceptional speed and leaped to their feet outside.

As soon as they stood up, someone pushed them back down. It was Robert and Charlotte. They tackled Boaz and Andrea to the floor, pushing them out of the way of a giant metal block that was hurdling at their heads. Their quick thinking saved their friends' lives.

Boaz and Andrea finally got a good look at the attacker. They gasped. Andrea dropped the bracelet in shock.

"No …" said Boaz in a quiet yet horrified voice.

The attacker was none other than Tyler, wearing the titanium Element Blasters that Boaz and his friends built for him.

*   *   *

"Tyler had betrayed us," Boaz continued. "In the past, he had tried to build his own Element Blasters but had been unsuccessful. My friends and I were the only ones who knew how to build them. Tyler abused our trust and alliance so he could get his hands on our technology and use it to take over the city."

"What happened next?" Steven asked cautiously. Even though this was his first time hearing this story, he already had a pretty clear idea of the events that followed. But that didn't stop him from asking.

Boaz paused for a moment. "Without our armor and Element Blasters, we were significantly overpowered. I managed to snag a pipe to counter Tyler's attacks while the others hurried off to the armory. I bought them less than a minute of prep time, but Tyler eventually kicked my weapon out of my hands and struck my right leg with a block of titanium that he wore around his hand. As I screamed in pain, he raised his fist for a finishing blow, but my friends returned with their Element Blasters and drew his attention away from me. I lay there in pain as the battle continued, but the outcome resulted in something much, much worse than the pain of my broken leg."

Another pause occurred as Boaz caught his breath. Though he didn't cry, Steven could see a thin layer of moisture forming in his father's eyes.

"Tarsus managed to short-circuit their Element Blasters. When he caught them off guard, he trapped them in a block of solid titanium. Then … then …"

Boaz shuddered. "He shoved them into an escape pod," he whispered sharply and slowly.

Steven felt his own tears come to him.

"And before I could even process what happened …" Boaz breathed through his teeth. *He blew it up.*"

The room was completely silent. No one said anything.

Boaz shuddered. "He killed them," he said solemnly. "I

knew him since I was a kid. I thought he was my friend ... *and he killed them!*"

The story was finally out. For years, Steven and Brooklyn had wanted to know exactly what happened during that space station battle which resulted in the end of the Table of Elements. But little did they know that it would be a story so personal to Steven. He now knew how his mother died and how his father had injured his leg.

"What ... what happened to Tarsus?" Brooklyn asked calmly.

Boaz sighed. "I managed to push him into an escape pod of his own and blasted him off into space."

Steven went cold. "You didn't ... *kill* him, did you?" he asked, desperately hoping the answer was no. To his relief, he was right.

"No," said Boaz. "As furious and despondent as I was, I would never take a life and disobey God. All the pods had been programmed in advance to travel to San Francisco when launched. I specified the coordinates to send him directly to the police station, but by the time I returned, neither Tarsus nor the pod were anywhere to be found.

"After the battle, I stayed on the station for a few days, recovering. I never resumed my role as Helium, and I don't see how I ever can, not with my leg impairment. I returned to the city alone, flooding my ship with tears, and Steven spent the rest of his childhood raised solely by me ... without his mother ... my wife ...."

As he had been saying this, he had pulled from his pocket the very bracelet he had given his wife and held it tightly.

Steven's eyes were moist with tears, but he did not cry. "Why didn't you tell me this before?" he asked his father in a low voice.

"Because I wanted to protect you from danger," said Boaz. "It wouldn't have been safe to share all this information with you at such a young age. And … I was depressed. I lost my best friends and my wife."

Boaz bowed his head and gently closed his eyes. "My sweet Andrea," he said in a hushed voice, which trembled slightly. He sniffled. "I'm sorry I couldn't save her, Steven. I miss her so much. I miss them all."

Steven got up from his chair and hugged his father tightly. "It's OK," he said.

Brooklyn and Chief Adams joined in. One big group hug later, the sadness went away. Acceptance took its place.

"To think all this time, that Table of Elements poster in my room was a picture of my parents," Steven said thoughtfully.

"How did you know about this?" Brooklyn asked her dad.

"Boaz told me a few years ago," said the Chief. "But we agreed not to tell you until the right time came."

"And what happened to the Table of Elements' suits?" Steven asked.

"I had them stored in our old hideout," said Boaz, "along with a spare each."

"Your *hideout?*" Brooklyn repeated.

"An old warehouse at the San Francisco pier," Boaz clarified. "I hadn't accessed it in years until earlier today."

"We went to retrieve *these,*" said Chief Adams.

Boaz and the Chief reached behind their chairs, and each picked up a large silver case with an encrypted lock. The men set them on the table before Steven and Brooklyn, who stared in awe at the symbols engraved in the finest silver on each case. The room's overhead light caused the briefcases to shine like a precious treasure.

Boaz unlocked both cases by typing in a four-digit code.

With two sharp clicks, the massive cases were unlocked. Boaz and Chief Adams turned the cases around so that they faced Steven and Brooklyn and carefully opened them. A motion-sensor light shined on them as the cases opened, giving them a perfect view of the contents. Inside were two of the four Table of Elements armors. One was royal blue, and the other was marble white.

"I tinkered with the suits an hour ago," Boaz explained. "They're functioning properly again."

Steven and Brooklyn couldn't help but stare. They couldn't believe they were seeing two official Table of Elements suits. They looked brand new, as though they had been made only yesterday by the greatest armorer in the world, one who also had a burning passion for science fiction, for that matter.

"The suits are heat-resistant, tear-resistant, and the armor is completely impervious to knives and other sharp, pointy things," Boaz explained. "Observe."

Boaz got up and grabbed a sharp knife from a kitchen drawer. He jabbed it at the torso of the suit, and the blade bent like an accordion without even making a dent in the armor.

"Woah!" said Steven, very impressed.

"The armor and cowls are even durable enough to withstand a fall from a five-story building without making so much as a dent," Boaz continued as he returned to the dining room and sat back in his seat.

"The armor is also painted with latex for further protection, which is why it looks a little glossy and is insulted with a shock-absorbent gel to make it impact resistant. However, even though the suits are impervious to high-voltage devices such as tasers, the Element Blasters can be shorted out when exposed to too much electricity. This a flaw we were never able to fix.

"As for the cowls, they are equipped with these special

lenses that keep the wind from drying out your eyes when flying or jumping far. The lenses also block the sun's glare, hide the wearer's eyes to further protect their identities, and give him or her night vision. That's why a Table of Elements member never needed a flashlight on the job. As for the utility belt, one of the pouches was used to contain our licenses and wallets, and the other, for a pair of handcuffs.

"I understand that this is a lot to take in. Do you have any questions?"

Steven thought of one right away. "Why are you telling us all this now?" he asked.

"The team and I wanted to pass on the mantle to future generations," Boaz replied. "We knew that we couldn't go on forever. There would come a time when San Francisco would be without its protectors. We wanted to pass the mantle on to *you* and perhaps a few friends."

Steven thought he was going to faint. Him? A superhero? He couldn't believe this was happening. Once again, he and Brooklyn were lost for words.

"We wanted to wait until the two of you were old enough to take up the responsibility needed to be superheroes," said the Chief. "Now that you're almost sixteen and mature enough to make the right decisions, we believe you two are ready."

"But we're not going to force you," Boaz added. "Are you willing to take up the mantle? Do *you* think you're ready?"

Steven did not need to think about it. He already had his answer. He had dreamed of being a member of the Table of Elements for years, and now that could actually become a reality for him. Steven visualized himself flying around the city with Brooklyn at his side, the two of them saving people from wildly extreme catastrophes. Not to mention, he had been wanting to make up for the bus accident he caused, and now he had his chance. Perhaps, Steven thought, if he became a Table of Elements member, everyone would think of him as a hero instead of the kid who caused the school bus to crash.

In the most confident voice he could muster, Steven stood up and said, "I'm ready, Dad."

Boaz looked pleased with his son's response.

Brooklyn stood up, too. She held Steven's hand. "If Steven's in, then I am, too," she said.

Steven and Brooklyn both stared down at their hands. Steven thought Brooklyn was blushing a bit, but she stopped holding his hand at once and looked back at Boaz and Chief Adams before he could tell.

"Your mother would be so proud of you," said the Chief with a smile.

"Yours, too, Steven," added Boaz. "It's settled then. Tomorrow, I will assign suits and teach you how to use your abilities. I'll be training you for the next two weeks."

"'Two weeks?' " Steven repeated. "But that's the entire Spring Break."

"We can't have you running around in those suits without practice," said Boaz. "The job you've taken up is dangerous work."

"OK," said Steven. "Wait, but … Dad? Chief? Is it legal for Brooklyn and me to be stopping crimes and helping people without a license?"

"Who's to say you won't have a license?" said the Chief. "The Table of Elements were licensed back when they first began. Once you complete your training, I'd be honored to deputize you two."

"Wow, that's great!" said Steven happily.

"We're proud of you two and excited to see you in action," said Boaz. "But remember—a hero doesn't do things for personal gain, but to serve God and to help people. Don't ever forget that."

"We won't," Brooklyn replied.

"Good," said Boaz.

"Now, I don't know about the rest of you," said Chief Adams, "but I think this calls for a victory meal. What do you say we go grab a pizza!"

"Oh, yeah!" said Brooklyn.

"Sounds great!" said Steven.

"I'll get my keys," said Boaz.

Boaz, Brooklyn, and Chief Adams headed to the foyer to grab their coats. Steven started in the same direction but changed his mind mid-step.

"I'll be right back, guys!" he announced.

Steven dashed up the stairs to his room, sat, and prayed.

"Thank You, Father! Thank You so much! If You are willing, please help us to bring You glory. Amen."

After closing, he grabbed his coat from his closet and headed back downstairs to join the people he loved for a celebratory pizza dinner.

CHAPTER SIX

SATURDAY, MARCH 13TH

TO SAY THAT Steven was happy it was Saturday would be an understatement. He was so excited that he hardly slept the night before. He still couldn't get over the fact that his parents had been part of the Table of Elements and that his childhood dream of becoming a member himself was actually going to come true. Finally, since it was Saturday, and Spring Break for that matter, he and Brooklyn had the whole day to practice.

After eating breakfast and washing the dishes, Steven and Boaz got into the latter's car and drove across town to the piers. They parked their car across the street from a large weather-worn warehouse at Pier 30 in the South Beach region of the city. Steven could see the iconic Bay Bridge not too far from where they were.

Steven and Boaz got out of the car and crossed the street. The morning was gray and gloomy. The seagulls were crying overhead, and the smell of the Bay, like a nautical air freshener, filled Steven's nostrils.

A few minutes later, Chief Adams arrived with Brooklyn. After the four of them said a group prayer, asking God to give them strength and guidance, Chief Adams drove off, leaving Steven and Brooklyn with Boaz.

"Are you guys ready?" Boaz asked with a smile.

"Yes!" the two of them exclaimed at once.

"Shhh!" Boaz said, still maintaining his grin. "This is a secret hideout. We can't draw any attention to ourselves!"

"Right, sorry!" said Steven, grinning with embarrassment. "Just excited."

"So, is there a key or something to get inside?" Brooklyn asked.

"No. No key," Boaz answered. "Just a bolt lock."

Boaz slid the small metal pillar out of the lock and opened the massive wooden door. Steven thought it was strange how easy it was to access the Table of Elements' hideout until Boaz showed them the inside. It was completely empty. There was no table, workbench, chair, or anything whatsoever in the warehouse. A little daylight seeped through the tiny square windows, though it was so little that it barely illuminated anything besides a small portion of the floor.

"*Ta-da!*" Boaz said heartily, throwing out an arm as though presenting a great work of art.

Steven couldn't think of any building that looked less like a work of art. He wasn't even sure if a "dumpster museum" would want this place on display. The wood was old, the paint was faded, and the structure was slightly crooked. He wondered if it would collapse if a seagull landed on the roof. Steven wouldn't have been surprised if it did.

"So ... *this* is the Table of Elements' hideout?" Brooklyn asked, sounding surprised.

"I was expecting something ... what's the word ... cooler?" Steven added, confused.

Boaz laughed. "This is just a cover," he admitted. "A decoy. The real hideout is *beneath us.*"

Boaz hobbled over to the front left corner and bent down. Grabbing hold of an iron handle, he lifted a wooden trapdoor built into the floor, which opened on hinges. Underneath *that* trapdoor was *another* trapdoor, which was sleek and made of metal, with a keypad instead of a handle. Boaz typed in a code, and the door unlocked and opened on its own.

"Ohhhhhh!" said Brooklyn, looking and sounding impressed by the clever deception.

Steven laughed a little. It made a lot of sense once he thought about it. An empty warehouse was a great disguise. It never would have crossed his mind that there was an entrance to a secret superhero hideout underneath.

Steven expected to find a ladder or something beneath the trapdoor. But instead, there was a smooth platform, large enough to hold five people.

"Come with me," said Boaz.

Steven and Brooklyn headed over to the corner and stood on the platform with Boaz, who pressed another button on the keypad. Moments later, Steven heard the whirring sound of hydraulics, and the platform lowered itself into the floor. It was an elevator!

In less than a minute, Steven, Brooklyn, and Boaz were about a hundred feet beneath the warehouse in a sleek, shiny, futuristic lair nearly three times the size of the warehouse above.

The place was lit up by blue digital lights, which hummed quietly as though they were in an airplane. The walls were pearly white and light gray, the same colors as the museum in the Presidio, and there was no dust or a single cobweb anywhere.

The hideout was still empty, just like the warehouse upstairs. However, after Boaz pulled a lever on the side of the wall closest to him, panels on the floor slid open, and various pieces of training equipment, including a bench press, treadmill, and several practice targets, emerged on elevator platforms of their own.

"This is amazing!" said Brooklyn.

"No way!" Something had caught Steven's eye—something iconic, futuristic, and capable of driving and flying. It was the real Regnier spaceship. "It's been here all this time," Steven said to himself.

"She's a beauty, isn't she?" said Boaz, patting the vehicle's hull as if it were a dog. "We had this built during our second year of crime fighting. It was a lot more effective than driving around in a refurbished ice cream truck."

"Are we going to be able to drive it or fly it?" Steven asked, hoping the answer was "yes."

"Not yet," said Boaz, shaking his head. "Brooklyn's father and I want to wait until you get your licenses first. Then, after thorough practice, I'll let you use the Regnier."

"Cool!" said Brooklyn. "I can't wait."

"Me neither. Let's get this party started!" said Steven, returning his thoughts to training.

"Hold your horses there, kiddo," said Boaz. "The first thing we need to do is assign suits."

Boaz pressed a button on the wall that was the size of his palm. The wall slid open like an elevator door to reveal the four cases containing the Table of Elements suits. All of them were neatly stacked like a plate of pancakes. Boaz and Chief Adams had returned the cases to the base the prior night after dinner.

Boaz gave Brooklyn the choice between the Silicon and the Beryllium suit. Steven wasn't the least surprised when she chose the former.

"Congratulations, Brooklyn," Boaz announced. "You are now the new wearer of the Silicon armor."

Brooklyn grinned ecstatically as Boaz handed her the case containing the Silicon suit. Steven had never seen Brooklyn look so happy with a gift before.

"Sweet!" she said. "Where … uh … is there anywhere for me to change?"

"There are four individual changing rooms on your left," Boaz pointed out.

"Thanks, Boaz," said Brooklyn, heading to one of the changing rooms with the case under her arm.

"Now, that leaves you, Steven," said Boaz. "Which suit would you like? I'll let you decide."

Steven didn't expect to think about the decision as long as he did, but the Lithium and Helium suits both seemed cool. He thought the Lithium suit would be electrifyingly fun, pun completely intended. He remembered seeing Robert use the amazing powers of lithium on TV, powering up broken power towers and destroying robots with his electric blasts. However, Steven preferred the Helium suit. He always thought it would be fun to fly. Besides, the Helium suit had belonged to his dad, so he felt an emotional attachment to it. Keeping these factors in mind, Steven made his decision.

"I'll take the Helium suit, Dad. I'd like to take up your mantle."

"Great choice," said Boaz. The twinkle in his warm eyes

told Steven that he was just as happy with the decision as he was.

Boaz handed him the case with the Helium suit inside. "It's all yours," he said.

But then, a concern came to Steven. "Will this be able to fit me?" he asked. "We don't exactly have the same body type."

"Not to worry, Steven. The armor and jumpsuit are completely adjustable. Press your utility belt's left button to make it smaller and the right to make it larger."

"Which left?"

"Your left," Boaz clarified. "Left-hand side."

Thanking his dad, Steven cheerfully dashed into another changing room and suited up. After pressing the left-hand button on his belt, the jumpsuit tightened to fit his build, the armor plates remodified themselves to make them smaller, and the suit fit perfectly. Indeed, the armor added about ten to twelve pounds to his weight, but Steven could still move freely. He could even move his neck as smoothly as he could without the armor since the cowl was a separate piece and not connected to the neck of the suit. Plus, the armor was also Steven's favorite color.

When he left the room, he found Brooklyn looking at herself in a mirror on the wall. Steven joined her, and she looked just as pleased with *her* outfit as he was with his. Even though their eyes could not be seen through the lenses of the masks, Steven and Brooklyn were pleasantly surprised to find that prosthetic lids would open and close, shielding the lenses as though they were eyelids, whenever they squinted or closed their eyes. They had a lot of fun practicing various expressions, trying to see all the different looks the eyes could make. Boaz and the rest of the team certainly put incredible work into making the suits.

"This is amazing!" said Brooklyn, putting her hands on her hips and giving a heroic grin. "We're the Table of Elements!"

"Yeah, this is a total dream come true!" Steven agreed. "You know, the armor is actually really comfortable. I think the boots are my favorite."

"I love the mask, personally," said Brooklyn. "It's very futuristic."

"I agree," said Steven. "And I can't wait to go on patrol with you, the two of us, side by side, protecting the city and fighting evil!"

"So, do you guys want to practice your *poses* or your *powers?*" Boaz asked from across the base.

Steven and Brooklyn turned away from the mirror and headed across the room until they were face-to-face with Boaz.

"Let's begin," Boaz announced.

SATURDAY, MARCH 27TH

Steven and Brooklyn trained in the secret hideout with Boaz for two weeks straight, from morning to evening. They worked harder than they ever worked in all their lives. Boaz had both of them practice using their Element Blasters and other special abilities until they had mastered them and could use their powers without hesitation. It helped that Boaz and the kids prayed every day for God to give them strength and perseverance. Finally, when Boaz told the kids they were ready, he took them to the mayor's office, and Chief Adams deputized them.

"I trust that you will use your powers to help people and protect our city," Chief Adams told them. "Be responsible and make smart choices. It's dangerous work out there."

Steven and Brooklyn saluted.

"We will, Dad," said Brooklyn.

He then handed them their official licenses. Steven had often longed for a driver's license and a car to go with it, but this *law-enforcement* license seemed better than driving the coolest car in the world.

"I'll admit it," said the mayor from behind his desk, "when Chief Adams here first told me that two high school sophomores were planning on taking up the mantle of the Table of Elements, I was very skeptical. But I trust him, *and* the original Helium"—he looked at Boaz—"and have faith that you will do a great job just like he and the rest of the team did. Mr. Starcluster, Miss Adams,"—the mayor paused as he saluted the duo—"I wish you the best."

"Thank you, sir," said Steven. "We won't disappoint."

"I believe you," said the mayor.

"God bless you both," said the Chief. "Helium and Silicon."

Steven and Brooklyn put their licenses in their wallets and their wallets in the left pouch of their utility belts. Then, they each put a pair of handcuffs, also given to them by Chief Adams, in their right pockets. This was the proudest moment of Steven's life. He was now a real Table of Elements member, just like he had always dreamed of. He couldn't wait to start patrol the next day. He was certain that he and Brooklyn would make an excellent team.

SUNDAY, MARCH 28TH

After church that morning, Boaz called Steven and Brooklyn to the roof of BRCA Apartments, announcing that they were now ready to go on their first patrol.

Steven and Brooklyn high-fived each other. "Yes!" they exclaimed.

"Where are we going to go?" Steven asked his dad.

"Wherever you want as long as you're back by four," Boaz answered. "Do you have everything?"

Steven and Brooklyn checked their belts. They both had their licenses and handcuffs. "Yes," they confirmed.

"Good," said Boaz. "Be safe and call me if there's anything wrong. But before I let you go, promise me you will not harm anyone except in self-defense."

"Yes, Boaz," said Brooklyn.

"We promise," said Steven.

"Great. Now, get out of here!" Boaz said with a playful grin.

Steven chuckled. "Yes, sir, *Your Majesty!*"

He stood on the building's ledge and stared down. It was about a four-hundred-foot drop. He took a deep breath and prayed for strength. Finally, after activating his Helium Boots, Steven jumped off feet-first and hovered in midair.

It was as though he were in a dream. Nearly everyone has dreamed of flying at some point in their life, and now Steven was experiencing it for real. Union Square looked like a toy model from his level, but the Square would have to wait because he and Brooklyn were eager to explore other parts of the city.

"What do you say we check out Fisherman's Wharf, partner?" Brooklyn asked.

"Sounds great ... *partner!*" said Steven.

Brooklyn lowered herself to the alley behind BRCA Apartments with a long and adhesive silicone rope. Steven flew to the ground and landed beside her.

"Let's move out!" he announced.

CHAPTER SEVEN

S TEVEN LED THE way as they
headed north on Mason Street
toward Fisherman's Wharf. Traveling sure was fun. He glided
a yard above the pavement like a large blue eagle surveying
the surface. Brooklyn's method of traveling wasn't as unique
as Steven's, but Steven thought it was impressive all the same.
Unable to fly, Brooklyn acquired a skateboard, which she
painted the other day to match the colors of her suit, and rode
it down the sidewalk, jumping over fire hydrants and swerving
around pedestrians and dogs. She was so quick and fluid in
her motions that she didn't even come close to hitting anyone
or anything. Even though he had known her for years, Steven
was still amazed when he saw her leap into the air, kickflip
before landing safely on the pavement, and continue to skate
alongside him.

A minute later, the teens reached the end of the street. They were now in the northeast region of San Francisco, right outside Pier 43. Beyond the pier was the beautiful San Francisco Bay. The weather was wonderfully cool, and the smell of saltwater and fried food filled the air. The place was appropriately crowded for a San Francisco morning, but Steven didn't see anyone from his school. This disappointed him—he had hoped for someone from Pine Tree High to see him in action—but he was still glad that there were any people at all.

Brooklyn kicked her board up and slid it into her thin black backpack before zipping it up.

"It's a good thing this armor's insulated," she said. "It's freezing!"

"It sure is," Steven agreed. "Still, first *day* on patrol, first *place* on patrol. This is going to be fun!"

"Definitely," said Brooklyn. "We better keep our eyes peeled."

This they did. Steven and Brooklyn observed their surroundings as casually as possible, which wasn't easy since they were wearing the Table of Elements' uniforms. But it wasn't long before Steven discovered an old lady and her husband on the corner of the street to his left. They seemed to be waiting to cross the street.

Steven gently tapped Brooklyn on the shoulder to get her attention. Once her eyes were locked on the couple, Steven said aloud, "Bingo."

Steven grinned and strolled over to the couple as if he was an average Joe on his way to work. Brooklyn reluctantly followed. She didn't seem too sold on the idea of approaching people as opposed to observing things from a distance.

"Hello, ma'am, sir," Steven said in a friendly voice.

The old couple gazed at the teens calmly. They didn't seem all that bewildered at the sight of their uniforms.

"Are you from a theatre group?" the old man asked in a languid, croaky sort of voice.

This was not the response Steven had expected, but he continued to smile.

"No, no, no," he answered cheerfully. "We're superheroes! We're the ... we're the ..." He turned to Brooklyn. "What are we called?" he whispered.

"'What are we called?'" Brooklyn whispered back, looking just as confused as the couple. "I don't know—"

"We're the 'I don't knows!'" Steven told the old couple before he could fully comprehend Brooklyn's response.

"You don't know what?" asked the old lady, sounding genuinely curious.

Steven hesitated. "Well ... I ... uh ... I don't know," he replied, feeling a little embarrassed.

"It sounds like you live up to your name," the old man retorted with a slight smirk.

"So, would you like any help crossing the street?" Steven asked.

"No, thank you," said the old lady, looking a little creeped out. "That's why we have the traffic light."

"Well, are there any crimes you'd like to report?" said Steven.

"Yes. *You*. Harassing us," answered the old man.

The light turned green at that moment, and the man and his wife crossed the street rather quickly, as though they were being chased.

"OK," Steven called out. "Well, thanks anyway!" The young hero sighed.

Brooklyn comfortingly placed her hand on his shoulder. "Don't listen to him," she said. "He was just being rude. But *you're* being too eager. We're supposed to be on patrol, so we just look at things from afar. We don't need to force ourselves into people's lives."

Steven had to admit that she was right. He probably would have been taken aback and creeped out, too, if someone like him had approached him like that, though he was sure that he would have been more polite than the man had been.

"You're right," said Steven. "I'm sorry. Let's get back to patrol. We have a lot of ground to cover."

"Right on, partner," said Brooklyn.

As they crossed the street, she asked, "Why didn't you tell them we were the Table of Elements?"

"When I thought about it, I thought it would be kind of weird," Steven admitted.

"Weird how?"

"Well, there's only two of us instead of four, and I've never heard of a two-legged table before."

Brooklyn laughed. "You've got to be kidding me," she said.

"No, really!" said Steven. "I thought maybe we needed a name change."

"I think we should just go with the Table of Elements for now," said Brooklyn. "It's iconic and catchy."

"I guess you're right," Steven agreed. "I was overthinking it."

"But who knows? Maybe we'll get a new member or two someday," said Brooklyn.

"Yeah, maybe ..."

*   *   *

Fisherman's Wharf was less exciting than Steven had hoped. Indeed, the scenery was colorful and fun to look at, and the sun had finally decided to come out and play, but there were no crimes to thwart and no people to save. The only times during the remainder of their visit that they interacted with anyone were when someone, thinking they were street performers, asked for a photo with their children, and when they stopped for lunch. They bought a couple of corndogs from a cart at Pier 39, and the lady selling them complimented them on their "costumes."

"Thanks," Brooklyn replied as she and Steven paid for their snacks, "but these are actually the genuine article."

"Really?" said the lady playfully, raising a brow to accommodate her grin.

"Yes, ma'am," said Steven. "We're the new Table of Elements."

The lady laughed as though she found them cute.

Steven was tempted to demonstrate his powers for her to prove himself but decided against it. He knew that it would make him seem like a show-off. Steven might have wanted to prove himself as a hero and a changed person, but he didn't want people to think that he was self-centered. He especially didn't want Brooklyn to have that kind of reputation, either. He cared about her too much.

Eventually, the teens traveled from Fisherman's Wharf to the Financial District in eastern San Francisco. This was a very active place with several tall and impressive buildings. Here, everything seemed smaller and cramped despite the buildings' large scale. People crowded the place like ants at a picnic. Cars, jackhammers, bike bells, and indistinct chatter were the most common sounds heard, and they were all very loud. Patches of grass, water fountains, and red, yellow, and white fire hydrants added to the colors of the district, which contrasted with the simpler colors of the buildings and skyscrapers.

Steven and Brooklyn sat on the steps of a building on the corner of Battery and Sacramento, watching the cars drive by. Nothing was out of place, and Brooklyn seemed happy about it. Steven, on the other hand, *wanted* something bad to happen so he could jump in and be the hero instead of sitting around in a superhero uniform which caused people to stare at him and Brooklyn.

"Why is everything OK right now?" Steven asked.

"What do you mean?" said Brooklyn.

"I mean that this is San Francisco—a very well-known city where many people live—and we've been out for hours now, and not one bad thing has happened. Where are all the crooks?"

"Maybe they're just in another part of town," Brooklyn suggested. "Or maybe they're all in jail."

"Well, at least everyone's OK," said Steven. He might have wanted to stop a crime, but he didn't want anyone to be in physical danger.

"Do you think we should move to another area?" Brooklyn asked.

Before Steven could answer, four thugs across the street tackled a man to the ground and snatched the huge bag he had been carrying. Before the man could get up and reclaim his belongings, the thugs hopped into a bright red, slightly dented convertible parked a few yards away and put the pedal to the metal. The car roared down the street like a bull gone mad and drove what seemed to be about three times the speed limit.

"Help!" cried the man. "They stole my stuff!"

Steven and Brooklyn leaped to their feet.

"Let's go!" Steven cried as he activated his Helium Boots.

Knowing that Brooklyn's skateboard would not be fast enough to catch up to the convertible, Steven sprayed her with helium so she could fly beside him.

It didn't take long for the two of them to reach the car, which hadn't slowed down in the slightest. The convertible was swerving from lane to lane, but thankfully, the street wasn't too busy. The few vehicles traveling on the road had managed to veer out of the way in time. Horns blared, adding to Steven and Brooklyn's stress about catching the crooks and stopping the car.

When the two of them were behind the convertible, Brooklyn latched two silicone lassos onto the back bumper. Unfortunately, in the heat of the moment, she had forgotten that she didn't have super strength. Because of this, when she stood her ground and pulled on the lassos as hard as she could, the silicone ropes lost their grip and shot back into her Element Blasters as the car sped away.

"What was I thinking?" Brooklyn roared in frustration.

"It's OK," said Steven.

Steven and Brooklyn continued to fly behind the car. The crooks in the convertible, who had just noticed them from their mirrors, looked stunned and horrified at seeing two teenagers with the powers of the Table of Elements following them in close pursuit.

"Floor it!" the crook in the passenger seat hollered to the driver.

The driver did what he was told immediately. The convertible might have been fast, but Steven and Brooklyn were quicker. They were still on their tail even with the convertible roaring down the street like a ferocious beast on wheels.

Steven fired several barrages of helium in the car's direction, but the driver swerved repeatedly to throw him off. Then, to Steven's shock, he discovered that the four crooks each possessed hand-held laser blasters, which they fired at him and Brooklyn in the air as if they were playing with housecats using laser pointers.

Brooklyn quickly formed a silicone shield to protect her and

Steven from the lasers. The one downside was that it made it extremely difficult for Steven to see where he was going.

"I can't see!" he told Brooklyn. "Blast a barrier in front of the car! We need to corner them!"

Brooklyn dropped the shield and did as Steven said. With her amazing powers, she blasted a silicone barrier several yards in front of the convertible, five feet high and a foot thick. The driver slammed the brakes so hard that the tires left skid marks on the street. Just as they were about to flip around and take off in another direction, Steven activated his Element Blasters. He sprayed as much helium as he could on the car, causing it to hover about six feet in the air, bobbing slightly like an apple in a pail of water. Steven could easily see the half-frustrated, half-scared crooks trying to floor the car out of the helium tractor beam, to no avail. The helium was much too strong.

"Yes!" Steven cried. "We did it!"

"All right!" said Brooklyn.

The duo landed and high-fived victoriously. After this, Brooklyn sprayed silicone on each of the convertible's wheels while the car was still hovering. Steven then lowered the car back to the street as three police cars arrived at the scene. The silicone prevented the criminals' convertible from driving off. As the police arrested the four crooks and led them to their cars, the officers kept glancing back at Steven and Brooklyn, their faces stunned.

"No way!" they heard one of them say.

"I was hoping to see the new Table of Elements soon," said another.

"They're a bit younger than I thought," said a third officer.

"Yeah, but they've still got skills!" said a fourth. "We've been chasing after this gang for weeks."

The two remaining officers were Chief Adams and his

partner, Xavier Barnes, a tall, slender man with flat hair and round glasses. He smiled like a child in a candy shop when he saw Steven and Brooklyn.

"Great work, kids," said the Chief. "Those hooligans have been causing us trouble for the past month."

"We're glad to have been of service … sir," said Brooklyn, who seemed to have caught herself before she called him "Dad."

"It's good to see you, Chief," said Steven.

"Likewise," said Chief Adams. "This is Officer Barnes. He's kind of a fanatic."

"Pleasure to meet you, sir," said Steven, shaking his hand.

Barnes looked ecstatic, as though he were shaking hands with a king. How he spoke made Steven assume he was trying to mask his childlike enthusiasm to stay professional while on the job.

"So, you're the new Table of Elements, huh?" he said casually, still shaking his hand.

"Yes, sir," said Steven pleasantly, looking down at their hands.

"Sorry," said Barnes, chuckling self-consciously as he pulled his hand away. "So, what are your names?"

Before Steven could answer, Chief Adams spoke up.

"Their identities shall remain secret, Xavier," he said. "The mayor and I have approved them, and they're licensed to enforce the law just as we are."

"We're not doing our job for attention, Officer," Brooklyn added. "Besides, we don't want to be stopped by crowds whenever we go out in public."

"I understand," said Barnes calmly. "It's nice to see people your age so humble and goodhearted."

Though he respected him, Steven was uncomfortable with what Chief Adams had said. How was he going to make it up to everyone back at school if they didn't know he was the new Helium?

Barnes, on the other hand, could not stop smiling.

"This is unbelievable," he said. "I was a huge fan of the original team, and I'm excited to see you two in action."

"Take care, kids," said the Chief, checking his phone. "We're needed back at the station."

Chief Adams and Officer Barnes returned to their car and drove off down the street as Steven and Brooklyn returned to the corner where the man who had been robbed was waiting patiently.

"Here you are, sir," said Steven, handing him his bag. "All your valuables are safe and sound."

Now that he was right in front of him, Steven realized that this man was none other than Reginald Gargon—the inventor he and Brooklyn met at the Table of Elements museum.

"You two are absolutely incredible! Thank you," said Mr. Gargon heartily.

"No problem, sir," said Brooklyn. "We were happy to help."

"This might sound like a silly question," Mr. Gargon continued, "but are you ... the Table of Elements?"

Clearly, he didn't recognize the duo from the day of the field trip since they were wearing masks this time.

Steven and Brooklyn beamed, placing their fists on their hips heroically.

"We are, indeed, sir," said Steven. "We're the new generation!"

"Well, it's a genuine pleasure to meet you," said Mr. Gargon politely. "My name is Reginald Gargon. And what might your names be?"

Brooklyn told Mr. Gargon their codenames as she and Steven took turns shaking his large hand. It felt kind of strange to introduce themselves to someone whom they had already met a couple of weeks prior.

"I respect your decision to keep your identities secret," said Mr. Gargon. "If I were as talented as the two of you, I wouldn't want to be swarmed by fanatics wherever I go, either."

"Well, we're not as awesome as the One who gave us our courage and strength," said Steven.

"You're still 'awesome,' all the same," said Mr. Gargon, making air quotes as he grinned. "Is this your first day?"

"Yes," said Brooklyn. "And it seems to be going very well."

"Well, I wish you the best with your new career," said Mr. Gargon politely. "I should get going now."

"Take care, sir," said Steven. "It was nice to meet you."

"Likewise," said Mr. Gargon, heading down the street with his bag over his shoulder.

As he did this, Steven and Brooklyn resumed their city patrol, laughing joyfully with one another. Things were going great.

CHAPTER EIGHT

LIKE CHIEF ADAMS, Boaz was also very pleased with the success of Steven and Brooklyn's first patrol. By the time the teens returned to BRCA Apartments, Boaz told them that they had been featured on the news and were trending like a new flavor of ice cream. Steven felt wonderful. He was so overjoyed that he thought his head might swell up like a balloon.

After dinner and a little TV, Steven got permission to put his suit back on as he relaxed on the roof of the building. Brooklyn, who had obtained the same consent from *her* father, joined him. They sat on the ledge with their legs dangling as they sipped glasses of lemonade through swirly straws and observed the sunset.

"This is great," said Steven. "Would you just look at that view? It's like a painting."

"True, true," said Brooklyn before taking another sip of her lemonade. "All in all, a pretty amazing end to a pretty amazing day. We got to go on our first patrol, watch *Zeke the Funniest,* and now watch this beautiful sunset together."

Brooklyn set her glass down behind the ledge before resting her hand. Little did she realize that Steven's hand was directly beneath hers, and she had just placed her hand on top of his.

Steven and Brooklyn's smiles disappeared in a snap the moment they, still looking straight ahead, felt the contact of their hands.

Steven's heart skipped a beat. Wait a minute … why *was* it skipping a beat? He had known Brooklyn since middle school. He shouldn't have been embarrassed by something like this. It was an accident. It was … why wasn't he moving his hand?

Why wasn't Brooklyn moving *her* hand?

Steven just sat there, not sure what to do. Was Brooklyn OK with their hands touching, or was she just too embarrassed to say anything? Wait a minute. Brooklyn, embarrassed? "Not in a million years!" Steven thought. Still, he felt like he had to say something but thought it best to play it cool, which wasn't easy for him.

"Brooklyn?"

"Yeah?" said Brooklyn, smiling slightly. She looked a lot more relaxed than Steven.

"I … uh … I think you're doing a … a great job … as a hero."

"Thanks. You … too."

A pause. They just looked at each other, not saying a word.

"I … um …" Brooklyn started.

Just then, she and Steven moved their hands, not because of how they felt about the situation, but because something peculiar had caught their eye on the streets below.

On the corner of Stockton and O'Farrell was the weirdest

robot Steven had ever seen. It had a body shaped like an upside-down bullet, with a cube for a head, two flexible metal tentacles for arms with claws at the end of them for hands, and two legs that were as high and thick as barrels. The robot was over ten feet tall and was approaching the jewelry store at the corner. Citizens were fleeing from it, some screaming, but the robot continued to trudge as slowly as a snail like it was the only thing there.

"Where do you think it came from?" Brooklyn asked.

"Not sure," said Steven. "And what would a robot want with jewelry?"

"Not sure," said Brooklyn. "Maybe it's stealing something for its master?"

"That could be possible," Steven replied. "Let's check it out!"

Steven powered up his Helium Boots and grabbed Brooklyn's hand, flying the two of them to the scene of the robot. As they approached, the robot, which hadn't seen them yet since it had its back turned, spun one of its claws-for-hands into a buzzsaw-type weapon and began to cut through the jewelry store's locked door.

Steven wasn't sure if the robot had a consciousness of its own or not but, thinking it would be best to try and talk with it instead of destroying it right away, he cleared his throat as loudly as he could.

The robot ceased sawing and swiveled its cubed head to look at Steven and Brooklyn with its camera lens-like eyes. Both the robot and the heroes froze as they made eye contact.

"Um … hello … sir," said Steven, unsure if this was the proper way to address it.

"'Hello, sir?' " Brooklyn repeated in a whisper, raising a brow.

"I was trying to be polite!" Steven whispered back.

"Let me try," said Brooklyn.

She spoke in a sharp, clear voice as she asked the robot, "Who sent you? State your business."

The robot did not seem to be a talkative machine. It swung its long tentacle arms, with buzzsaws still at the end of them, at Brooklyn and Steven, who leaped over them like they were playing jump rope.

"I'll take the front!" said Steven. "You take the right!"

"What?" said Brooklyn, who hadn't heard over the commotion of the fight.

"The *robot's* right!"

"It's right about what?"

"Never mind!" cried Steven. "Just help me tie it up!"

Brooklyn sprayed silicone at the robot's feet to hold it in place. Then, she sprayed some more in the form of a long, solid rope. She tossed it to Steven, who flew over the robot and wrapped the rope around it repeatedly until it was wrapped like a present. However, it didn't take the robot long to rip through the silicone like spaghetti. As Brooklyn sped over to it, the silicone went flying off the robot and wrapped around Brooklyn, causing her to fall to the street, stuck to it like glue.

Suddenly, the robot wrapped one of its tentacle arms around Steven's torso and arms. Steven choked as the bot squeezed him like a boa constrictor. His sight blurred as he felt his life being squeezed out of him. As if that wasn't bad enough, the robot reactivated its buzzsaw hand and moved it closer and closer to Steven, whose heart pounded rapidly as he struggled to escape.

Thankfully, Brooklyn freed herself at that very moment, formed a giant mallet from silicone, and smashed it as hard as she could into the robot's back. The robot loosened its tight grip, and Steven was able to wriggle himself out before flying as fast as he could into the air.

"Thanks!" he cried.

"Anytime, dude!" said Brooklyn, drawing her mallet back to take another swing at the robot.

The mechanical villain was ready for her this time and grabbed hold of the mallet a second before it could smash its body. Brooklyn and the robot struggled before the former eventually let go and slid like a ball player under the robot's legs. On the other side of the robot, Brooklyn blasted a lasso around the robot's arms and middle and pulled as hard as she could. Brooklyn shot Steven a look that let him know now was the time to act.

Seeing this opportunity, Steven nodded at Brooklyn and activated his Element Blasters, spraying helium on a nearby boulder. Still flying, Steven did a backflip in midair and kicked the boulder toward the robot. The boulder smashed right into the robot's head, and electric sparks crackled as the mechanical foe powered down and collapsed to the ground. Brooklyn let go of her lasso after seeing that the robot was defeated. Steven deactivated his boots and landed beside his friend, gasping for breath.

"Great job," Steven complimented. "You were amazing!"

"So were you," Brooklyn returned with a weary grin.

The two of them eyed the vanquished robot as they caught their breath.

"Well, we should probably get this to the police," said Brooklyn.

"Hey, look," Steven said, pointing to the police car that was pulling up beside them.

"Wow. Right on time," said Brooklyn.

Two police officers exited the car and approached Steven and Brooklyn cautiously. Steven recognized them from the day he and his dad talked with Chief Adams at the police department. They were Officer Johnson and Officer Avril.

"Woah!" Officer Johnson exclaimed with a star-struck look. "Stan was right—the Table of Elements *are* back!"

Officer Avril observed the robot in the middle of the street. "Is this the robot we got a call about?" she asked the heroes.

"Yes, ma'am," Brooklyn answered. "I think Helium crushed its power source."

"What was it trying to do?" asked Officer Johnson.

"We found it sawing through the store's front door," Steven explained, pointing to the place over his shoulder with his thumb. "But we're not sure what its purpose was."

"Interesting," said Officer Johnson.

Officer Avril bent down on one knee to further examine the robot.

"I'm not a robotics expert," she admitted, "but the circuitry looks advanced. Way beyond anything I've ever seen."

"Same here," Officer Johnson added. "That's a pretty big boulder you threw at its head, though. We'll need the one responsible to remove it so we can preserve the machine."

"Yes, sir," said Steven.

He immediately used his helium to pull the boulder out of the robot's head and returned it to the other side of the street where he had found it. Then, he sprayed the robot with helium and gently laid it down on top of the police car. Brooklyn used silicone to keep the body from sliding off.

The officers were impressed.

"I never thought I'd see the day when the Table of Elements returned to help the city again," said Officer Avril with a cool smile. "Great work."

"Thank you, officers," said Steven and Brooklyn together.

The two officers saluted them before returning to their car.

As they drove off, a swarm of people, who had been watching the fight from a distance, started cheering and applauding Steven and Brooklyn. It was a terrific feeling. The teens thanked everyone before returning to their building the long way so no one would find out where they lived.

As Steven returned to the penthouse, changed into his pajamas, and crawled into bed, he couldn't help but praise God for the amazing day he had, and he couldn't wait to see what events the next day would bring him at school. Would everyone forgive him, or would all his work as a superhero have been for nothing?

CHAPTER NINE

MONDAY, MARCH 29TH

S TEVEN'S ALARM WENT off at seven o'clock that morning. Eagerly, he hopped out of bed and completed his morning routine before racing down the stairs like a horse out of its pen.

"Finally!" he thought. "Everyone's going to know that I'm a superhero now! I'll be able to tell them all about Brooklyn and me stopping a band of criminals in a getaway car and defeating a robot! I wonder if they've heard about it yet. Regardless, everyone will finally forgive me after hearing about all the heroic things that Brooklyn and I have done!"

As he reached the dining room, Steven found Boaz sitting at the table, sipping tea and eating a bowl of oatmeal. The radio was on in the kitchen at a low volume, playing some classical jazz. When Boaz saw Steven, he put down his spoon and swallowed before he spoke.

"Good morning," he said, sounding like he was trying his hardest not to laugh.

"Good morning," Steven returned.

Then, to both his surprise and confusion, his dad started cracking up. It started soft and quiet before growing into uncontrollable hysterics.

"Wh-what's so funny?" Steven asked, feeling like laughing, too.

Boaz wiped his eyes and took a deep breath. "Oh, kiddo!" he said. "I'm so sorry! School's been canceled."

Steven froze. " 'Cancelled?' " he repeated.

Boaz pointed to his laptop. "Yeah, I got an email from the principal. There was a flood last night. The school is soaked. It won't be opened again until tomorrow. Sorry that you got all dressed this early for nothing, but hey! An extra day off!"

A *flood?* Steven was trying to think of how this could have happened. Did a janitor leave a sink on overnight? Did the pipes break? The building was over fifty years old, after all.

"Why don't you go back to sleep?" Boaz suggested. "I've got to get ready for work soon."

"OK," said Steven nonchalantly with a small, forced smile.

He gave his dad a quick morning hug before heading back upstairs. His grin dropped when he closed his bedroom door behind him.

Tomorrow.

Never before had that word sounded so terrible and depressing. Now he would have to wait another day to tell everyone at school about his new identity. Steven wanted to be angry but knew that it was not the right way to react. After all, it was only one more day. He instead chose to be thankful that it was so close. And to be honest, he found it kind of nice to have another day off, especially after he wiggled under his covers and sunk his head back into his pillow.

He awoke again an hour later after Boaz had left for work. He talked on the phone with Brooklyn, who asked him if he had heard about the school flood.

"Yeah, it's weird," he answered. "A building learned how to rain indoors."

"Seriously though," said Brooklyn over the phone, "how do you think it could have happened?"

"I don't know," said Steven. He shrugged his shoulders even though Brooklyn couldn't see him. "Sprinkler malfunction? Whatever it is, at least we got another day of patrol ahead of us."

"Aw, yeah!" said Brooklyn. "I'll meet you on the roof in fifteen minutes."

"Sounds great," said Steven. "Where should we go? Fisherman's Wharf?"

"Nah, I love the wharf, but we've already been there."

"OK," said Steven coolly. "What do *you* suggest?"

"How about the Golden Gate Bridge? Where better to patrol than the most iconic scene in San Francisco?"

Steven was sold. "Perfect!" he said. "See you in a bit."

*   *   *

It had been a while since Steven and Brooklyn last walked across the Golden Gate Bridge. Steven still vividly remembered the first time Boaz had taken him there. The two of them walked across it and back, and little Steven had been so young that Boaz eventually had to give him a piggyback ride halfway across the second trip.

This visit was quite different from the one Steven reminisced about. He and Brooklyn hiked across the bridge more slowly than the typical walkers, keeping their eyes peeled behind their masks for any suspicious activity. However, there appeared to be nothing criminal occurring at the moment, and it didn't help that a parade of Table of Elements fans, who'd discovered the duo while hiking the bridge, were now mobbing them like they were royalty.

At first, Steven was happy about the positive attention, but after a while, he became irritated and found it much harder to walk. Thankfully, some of the fans were kind enough to let him and Brooklyn through.

"It's hard to see with everyone here," Brooklyn said over the clamoring crowd. "I wish they'd stop asking us to pose for pictures."

"Don't worry, partner," said Steven positively. "Our solution seems simple."

"What's the solution?"

Steven looked up the first Golden Gate Tower as far as he could.

"We can just head to the top of the tower and survey the bridge from there," he proposed.

Brooklyn inhaled through her teeth. "I don't think that's a good idea, dude."

"How come?" Steven asked.

Brooklyn pointed to the sign next to the tower's ladder— "Authorized personnel only."

"Oh," said Steven. "Well, we'll find another way. And it sounds like the crowd's getting louder. It sounds like screaming …."

"That's not the crowd, dude," said Brooklyn, peering over the side of the bridge. "Look!"

Steven turned away from the tower and gazed in the direction that Brooklyn was looking. He gasped. Out in the middle of the San Francisco Bay was a man yelling for help. He looked like he was drowning.

"Oh, no!" Steven cried. "We need to help him! Can you make a boat or something out of silicone?"

"I can try," said Brooklyn.

Steven watched as Brooklyn formed a large, flat, square-shaped object that looked more like a container lid than a boat. Thankfully, she told him that it would be strong enough to hold their weight.

The duo climbed aboard the raft. Then, Steven sprayed it with helium and raised it in the air a little before lowering it to the water as if it were attached to a parachute. Steven stood on the back of the raft, stuck his arms out in front of him, and blasted more helium out of his Element Blasters, propelling him and Brooklyn toward the drowning man, whom they reached in record time.

"Don't worry, sir!" Brooklyn called out. "We're here to rescue you."

Just then, the man pulled his entire head out of the water and cried out in a frightened voice: *"Behind you!"*

Steven and Brooklyn spun around and came face-to-face with a frightening silver object rising from the waters, three feet in diameter and longer than the largest snake in the world, only bigger around. It was hard to tell the exact length, considering that half of it was underwater, but it looked like an octopus tentacle made of metal.

The robot tentacle sat upright like an angry snake, ready to strike. With a *WHISH!* the tentacle shot forward. Steven tried to duck, but the tentacle was too fast, knocking him like a ragdoll off the boat. Steven powered up his Helium Boots and blasted into the sky, narrowly avoiding the icy waters.

Brooklyn jumped forward, shot an adhesive silicone rope at

the robot, and tugged on it like a cowboy with a lasso, reeling it in to keep it from moving.

"I'll hold it down!" Brooklyn shouted. "Get the man in the water to safety!"

"Ten-Four!" said Steven.

Steven swooped down like a bird and pulled the man out of the water. As fast as his boots could go, Steven dropped him off on the soft green grass of a nearby field. The poor man was drenched from head to toe and shivering. Steven could hear his teeth chattering.

"I'm sorry, but I've got to help my partner," Steven told the man. "I don't have a towel, but maybe you can do pushups and jumping jacks to warm up. I'll be back. I promise."

Steven returned to the battle in the Bay and discovered that Brooklyn had glued the tentacle down to the raft. But as soon as she did this, the tentacle's other end sprang up from the water and swept both heroes off the raft with a single strike. Steven sprayed helium on Brooklyn to stop her from plunging into the water.

Suspended in the air, Brooklyn formed a long, thin, ax-like blade out of silicone and cut the robot from the raft. The tentacle shot upward like a catapult, and the raft splashed back onto the surface of the water, now detached from the robot.

"I have a plan!" Steven exclaimed as he lowered Brooklyn to the raft.

He returned to the sky and, using his Element Blasters, sprayed a barrage of helium on the tentacle, which caused it to rise about twenty feet above the water. That's when he noticed something intriguing about the machine they had been fighting. The tentacle wasn't *part* of a robot; it *was* the robot. Now that he could see the whole thing, he realized the robot more closely resembled a snake than an octopus tentacle.

"Silicon! Now!" Steven told Brooklyn, spraying her with helium again.

Brooklyn was raised about thirty feet in the air almost instantly and speedily formed a giant silicone mallet. Then, once the robot was directly below her, she used her creation to break the robot in half. The snake lost power as it splashed into the water. Steven gathered as many of the robot's pieces as possible and slid them onto the raft.

"We'll deliver these to the police to look over, but they'll probably have to get a scuba diver to retrieve the rest," he explained.

"How's the man?" Brooklyn asked.

"As far as I'm concerned, he's safe," said Steven. "We better go check on him, though."

Steven propelled the raft to shore and docked it near the field. He was happy to see that the man looked all right. He seemed to have taken Steven's advice because the duo could see him exercising.

When the man saw that Steven and Brooklyn had returned, he approached them calmly with a grin of relief stretched across his face as though he had just returned from a spa.

He shook both of their hands as he said, "How nice to see you again!"

Steven suddenly recognized him. It was Mr. Gargon yet again.

"Mr. Gargon! What a pleasure," said Steven.

"Thank you for the help," said Mr. Gargon.

"Happy to have been of service. And what are the odds of running into you again?" said Brooklyn with a smile.

Mr. Gargon chuckled. "What, indeed? So, how is your second day on the job treating you?" he asked.

"So far, so good," said Steven. "But how did you end up in the Bay?"

"Pardon me, please, but I'd very much like to warm myself back home," Mr. Gargon replied. "Would you care to join me for an early lunch? I never have visitors, and I can tell you my story there."

Though they hardly knew him, Steven and Brooklyn did not want to be rude and were curious to know how he ended up in that situation. So, they followed him across the field until they reached a hill at the back end.

CHAPTER TEN

"HERE'S MY FRONT door," Mr. Gargon pointed out.

An old door, camouflaged as part of the hill, was built right into the center of the area's back end. Steven wouldn't have even known it was there had Mr. Gargon not pulled on the slightly rusted handle and swung the door open. He escorted the heroes inside.

The floor was made of concrete, and the walls and ceiling were of dirt, with a few pebbles and roots sticking out here and there. Steven was very impressed by the interior. It astonished him, too, to see that the ceiling wasn't collapsing despite being made of dirt. He and Brooklyn followed Mr. Gargon through the hall until he led them down some steps into a room on the right.

There was one couch in the room, large enough for three people to sit on. Mr. Gargon, still wet from the Bay, stood under an air vent sticking out of the wall. He pushed a button, and a gush of air as loud as a jet engine exploded from the vent. Seconds later, Mr. Gargon shut off the vent and stepped out, as dry as a bone.

"Much better," said Mr. Gargon. "Would you care for a snack and some water?"

"That would be nice. Thanks," said Steven.

Mr. Gargon turned to a crooked wooden cupboard in the far corner of the room and pulled out three glasses. He ran them through a sink and returned with a wooden tray with three glasses of water and a loaf of sliced bread. The bread was a little stale, but to be polite Steven and Brooklyn ate it anyway.

"So, how did you end up in the water?" Brooklyn asked.

"Amusing anecdote, really," said Mr. Gargon with a gentlemanly chuckle. "I was testing my new robot out in the water when it went amuck and grabbed me from the shore."

"You built that snake?" Steven asked.

"Yes, indeed," Mr. Gargon confirmed. "I do have a knack for inventing, though I don't like to brag. That bag you reclaimed for me the other day was filled with little do-dads and scrap metal I planned to use for more machines and devices."

"What else have you invented?" Steven asked, very invested in the topic. He had been wondering whether or not he had ever gotten around to building that robot he mentioned on the day of the field trip.

"Why don't I show you?" Mr. Gargon suggested.

Steven and Brooklyn followed him out of the room and down the hall until they reached an even larger space. There appeared to be a furnace, various computers, workbenches, and even what looked like a giant mech-suit of some sort, eighty feet tall and huddled up in the corner of the room. But the mech didn't look ready for use since it had no shell.

In the center of the room was a real *spaceship*. It wasn't as sleek or cool as the Regnier, but Steven and Brooklyn were still impressed.

"I take it you like it?" said Mr. Gargon coolly.

"Very," said Brooklyn.

"How long did it take you to build this? It's amazing!" Steven exclaimed.

"One month," answered Mr. Gargon.

"How fast can it go?" Brooklyn asked.

"Its maximum speed is fifteen lightyears per hour."

"Nice," said Brooklyn.

"What made you decide to build a spaceship?" Steven asked.

"I've always had a great interest in astronomy," said Mr. Gargon. "Space interested me at a very young age and still does to this day. I was desperate to know if anything else lived out there besides us. What other planets or stars could there be? I wanted answers. I wanted to discover things. About a month ago, I went into space, keeping a journal to document everything I saw and taking pictures of my discoveries with my camera."

"What did you discover?" Steven asked.

"At first, nothing," Mr. Gargon replied. "That's why I spent the next two weeks in a space station with all my resources available. Of course, space stations aren't exactly the most common things to find, so I stayed in the one that the Table of Elements used to use. It made my stay more ... 'fascinating,' so to say, knowing that I was stepping foot in a place once occupied by the city's great heroes.

"Then one day, as I was testing my latest inventions, I was ambushed by a group of astronauts, who stole them from me and locked them inside the station. Thankfully, I was able to escape, but—" He sighed. "—I lost my wonderful inventions."

"I'm sorry to hear that," said Brooklyn.

"Maybe we can help you make some new ones," Steven suggested. "Did you keep any blueprints or instructions?"

Mr. Gargon shook his head. "My inventions' power sources are scarce. They cannot be found anywhere in this state or even this country for that matter. The best choice would be to retrieve the ones that were stolen from me."

Brooklyn lit up with excitement. "What about your spaceship?" she asked. "You could just fly to the station and get your inventions."

"If it were that simple, I would have done it the day I lost them," said Mr. Gargon. "It didn't take long upon my return to discover that I could not enter the station. Apparently, the leader of the astronauts had managed to snatch a strand of my hair and used it to devise a forcefield to prevent me from entering. Anyone else can come and go just fine. The forcefield only applies to me. Not to mention, I heard him and his team discussing the different defense systems they set up in my short time of absence. They even referenced posting a guard."

"What kind of guard?" Steven asked.

"I'm not sure," said Mr. Gargon. "But they said that he moves around the station in the blink of an eye and is nearly impossible to catch. Considering how they talked about him, he seems to be a dangerous force to be reckoned with. And he's surrounded by a series of highly advanced security measures such as a laser gate and a motion-sensor alarm system. To put it simply … I'm in a real jam."

"Why don't *we* go to the station and get your inventions back?" Steven suggested the moment it came to him.

"What?" said Brooklyn and Mr. Gargon at the same time, though their tones differed. The former seemed shocked at the proposal, while the latter looked delighted.

"Are you sure?" said Mr. Gargon. "It will be far from simple. As I mentioned, the station is heavily guarded."

"My partner and I can handle it," said Steven. "After all, we defeated two robots lickety-split. This should be a piece of cake!"

"Well ..." Brooklyn started with a look of hesitation.

"The space station is about four and a half lightyears away in the Srilvakor solar system," Mr. Gargon interjected. "With my ship's speed, the flight should only last about seventeen minutes. If the two of you are up to the task, I would be more than happy to fly you there. The mission should only take about an hour to complete, including the round trip."

"That sounds good!" said Steven.

He turned to Brooklyn.

"What do you say, Silicon? Are you up for an outer-space adventure?"

Brooklyn didn't look too sold on the proposal. Instead of answering Steven, she directed her attention to Mr. Gargon and asked politely, "May we please have a minute to discuss?"

"Certainly," said Mr. Gargon. "Take as much time as you need."

"Thank you," said Brooklyn.

She and Steven stepped out into the hall, where they could talk privately. Steven was filled with excitement.

"We'd have to be out of our minds to turn down this offer!" he said.

"Or wise," said Brooklyn.

"What do you mean?"

"We just met this man, dude," Brooklyn explained. "Besides, space is far and dangerous. We've never had anything even *close* to astronaut training. Helping a stranger is one thing, but going with him on a mission *lightyears* away from Earth is something else. I'm not sure we should do this."

Steven was not going to stand for that kind of talk. As far as he knew, doing this would be the coolest, most heroic thing he had done. If he did this, everyone would probably see how brave he was, and they would just *have* to forgive him. He pictured in his head Mr. Gargon, now reunited with his inventions, as a successful scientist living in a penthouse in the city. At the same time, the students and faculty of Pine Tree High cheered Steven and Brooklyn, who were publicly known to have completed this great task.

"We're sorry, Steven!" they cried. "You're a real hero!"

Confidently, Steven said aloud, "It will be all right, Brooklyn. We've defeated two robots and stopped a band of thieves the other day. We can easily handle something like this! By the time we return from the mission, Mr. Gargon will have his inventions back and show them to the public, and both your dad and my dad will be proud of the great deed we've done."

"I don't know, dude ..." said Brooklyn, bearing a look of uncertainty.

"We'll only be gone an hour," Steven reminded her. "Maybe less. That's not so long. Come on, Brooklyn! Isn't it important to help people? Isn't that what being a hero is all about?"

Brooklyn looked at Steven indecisively. "Are you *sure* it's the right thing to do?" she asked.

"Positive," Steven answered. "We're helping someone in need. So, what do you say?"

Brooklyn looked like she was solving a ten thousand-piece jigsaw puzzle in her head. Finally, she sighed and said, "All right. I'm with you, partner."

After Steven and Brooklyn informed Mr. Gargon of their decision, the latter announced they would leave in about ten minutes after he checked the ship's engines and packed some water and rations. The rations, it turned out, were more of the stale bread. Steven hoped the mission wouldn't last longer than the estimated time. The bread had left a not-so-pleasant taste in his mouth, and he was really not looking forward to eating more of it. The look on Brooklyn's face assured him that she wasn't very pleased with the food choice either.

Ten minutes later, Steven, Brooklyn, and Mr. Gargon climbed into the spaceship through a thick, vault-like door. The kids stared in awe. The interior looked like they stepped onto a set from a science fiction film. It was silver, with primary color buttons and wires, and dim, baby blue, digital lights that, like a washing machine, hummed softly.

There certainly were many buttons and switches on the control panel that Mr. Gargon was using. He pressed several buttons, flipped a few switches, and pulled down one lever, and the ship sprang to life. Steven could hear the engines roar.

It was then that he noticed Mr. Gargon looked kind of nervous. Brooklyn must have noticed, too, because she asked, "Are you OK, sir?"

"I'm f-fine," said Mr. Gargon. "It's just … it's been a while since I've been up there. I'm not used to flying. It's always a bit scary getting back into your comfort zone. Especially when you're about to rocket out of the atmosphere fifteen times faster than light."

Now that he had brought it up, Steven started feeling a little worried, too. Perhaps this hadn't been such a good idea after all.

In the bravest voice he could manage, Steven asked, "Since you've already been to space, do you think you could tell us what to expect? Launching, I mean?"

Mr. Gargon tapped his chin in thought.

"Well, you'll feel like your gravity has increased because

you'll practically be glued to your seats as the ship takes off. Imagine the fastest roller coaster you've ever been on, only much, much faster. Your ears might clog or pop, and the ship will rumble like an avalanche until it breaks through the Earth's atmosphere. This will last a few minutes, then it will all be still and quiet as we reach space."

Steven wasn't nervous anymore—he was *terrified*. Brooklyn had a look of fear in her eyes for a second before she closed them and took a deep breath. When she opened them again, she looked much calmer and braver, like she was ready to ski down the steepest mountain in the world. Part of Steven wanted to leave the ship and go home, but he prayed to God for courage and took a few deep breaths to calm himself.

He and Brooklyn then buckled their seatbelts before the former said quietly, "Let's do this."

Mr. Gargon, seeing that they were all buckled in, pressed a large round button on his control panel. There was a rumble above them, and the ceiling opened like a window, revealing the partly cloudy sky.

Mr. Gargon flipped two more switches, and the spaceship slowly tilted upward until its nose was pointed directly to the sky at a ninety-degree angle. With the ship prepped for launch, Mr. Gargon began the countdown. Steven and Brooklyn grabbed each other's hands and squeezed their eyes shut.

KABOOM!!!

Within seconds, the spaceship erupted from the room faster than Steven could have imagined. He sank deep into his seat, sweat piling on his face. He had never felt so uncomfortable in his entire life. He and Brooklyn kept holding hands.

Finally, when he felt he could no longer take it, everything suddenly stopped. His head launched forward like a boulder out of a catapult. Everything was so peaceful and silent that Steven could hear his eyelids blinking. It was a remarkable feeling. He had never heard such silence before. It was beautiful and also unnerving in a way, as though he had somehow escaped reality. The silence captivated Steven so much that it took him a while to acknowledge that it had grown significantly darker. Not to mention, stars could be seen from the spaceship's cockpit window.

"Children," said Mr. Gargon, "welcome to space."

CHAPTER ELEVEN

S TEVEN COULD NOT believe that he was in space, yet there he was—inside a real spaceship, surrounded by stars and silence.

"You can unfasten your seatbelts and walk around if you'd like," Mr. Gargon announced. "I've activated the artificial gravity."

It felt strange for Steven and Brooklyn to unbuckle their seatbelts without floating around the cabin. The artificial gravity feature worked perfectly, and they could walk around as if they were still on Earth. However, as the ship was small, there was little room to walk. Steven and Brooklyn would have gotten bored with this if it hadn't been for the breathtaking view through the porthole-like windows on the side of the ship.

"Enjoying the view?" Mr. Gargon asked from his seat.

"Oh, yeah. Definitely!" said Brooklyn.

"You'll never look at the night sky the same way after admiring stars up close like this," said Mr. Gargon.

"So, what was it like working in the Table of Elements' space station?" Steven asked casually.

"It was wonderful, really," said Mr. Gargon. "Very peaceful, very quiet, but also ... depressing at the same time."

"'Depressing?'" Steven repeated.

"Because you were lonely?" Brooklyn asked.

"No, rather because it was the last place where the Table of Elements were united," said Mr. Gargon. "It was a real shame what happened to them. Betrayed by someone who gained their trust. I was optimistic for Mr. Tarsus to join the team. I thought he would make a great addition."

"Did you know him?" Brooklyn asked.

Mr. Gargon paused. He looked uncomfortable.

"I did," he answered, sounding like he was reliving a bad memory. "It's strange. He never seemed evil or even all that mischievous. I was horrified when I watched the surveillance footage on the station of ... you know .... I never would have thought he'd be the one to turn against his friends ... to *kill* them."

"Mr. Gargon?" Steven interjected. "You don't ... you don't think Tyler Tarsus could be the guard on the station, do you?"

"I haven't thought of that," said Mr. Gargon. "He *could* be. He certainly would be a formidable foe."

Steven's heart sank. It made sense. A gang of ruthless astronauts had attacked Mr. Gargon and invaded his space station, and now they had someone posing as a guard at said station? Tyler Tarsus had never been found. As far as Steven knew, Tarsus could have crashed on another planet and formed a gang of spacemen to rob inventors of their technology. But would Steven be brave enough to face him—the man who killed his mother? How would he react?

Despite his mixed emotions, Steven confidently knew that he would never want to fatally harm anyone—not even someone as evil as Tarsus. If Tarsus was posing as a guard, he and Brooklyn would find a way to capture him and turn him into the police back home after they retrieved Mr. Gargon's inventions. The good news was that Steven didn't know if Tarsus was on the space station or not, and he really hoped he wasn't.

Several minutes later, a beeping noise came from the control console. Mr. Gargon spun around in his chair to check it out. His face lit up like a lightbulb.

"We've arrived in the Srilvakor system!" he said eagerly. "Quickly! Strap yourselves in."

Steven and Brooklyn hopped back into their seats and buckled up.

Seconds later, a massive space station came into view. It was shaped like an upside-down pie plate and was roughly the same size as Union Square. Its colors consisted of silver, copper, and purple.

Mr. Gargon flew the ship down to a landing pad. He turned off the engines as a glass tunnel shot out of the station's entrance and attached itself to the ship's door.

"I'll wait here," Mr. Gargon announced. "The inventions will be inside a brick-shaped metal container on top of a pedestal. Be careful."

"We will," said Brooklyn.

"See you in a bit, sir," said Steven.

The duo exited the ship and dashed through the glass tunnel. Like the spaceship, the gravity in the station was also equal to Earth's, which meant that they could walk and run just like they could back home.

They soon reached the station's entrance at the end of the tunnel. Steven and Brooklyn hesitated. They couldn't see the forcefield; Steven assumed it was invisible. When he stuck out his hand, it successfully passed through the entrance. Smiling at his success, he entered the space station with Brooklyn following.

"Wow! This is exactly how I pictured it would look," said Brooklyn when she and Steven arrived in the foyer, which was large enough to fit two whole floors of BRCA Apartments.

The entire interior was overflowing with vibrant orange, blue, and violet colors which gave the station a strong toy-like feel. The windows (their glass must have been at least three inches thick) were enormous and bolted into purple, octagon-shaped, metal frames. Like a summer breeze blowing through a tree, a low humming noise filled the station, and the dim lights bathed the interior in a soothing, yet exciting glow, similar to the dimmed lights of a movie theater which stir anticipation in a viewer.

But as impressive as the station was, Steven was having a hard time acknowledging it. Color left his heart-shaped face, and he was struggling to look up.

Brooklyn noticed. "Dude, what's wrong?"

Steven didn't move. "This is where my mother died," he said quietly.

Brooklyn comfortingly placed her hand on his armored shoulder. "Are you going to be all right?" she asked.

Steven paused before looking at his friend. "I think so," he said. "Y-yeah." He smiled slightly at Brooklyn, who smiled back in return.

"This place is huge," said Brooklyn. "Where do we start looking?"

Steven scanned the area until his eyes fell upon a nearby computer. "Maybe we can access *that*," he suggested.

Steven and Brooklyn approached the computer. More accurately, it was a computer *screen*, built directly into the wall and was the same size and shape as an American flag. Seeing that there was no physical button, Steven tapped the screen, and it soon came to life. A digital recreation of the space station appeared. Steven and Brooklyn played around with the map until they discovered a room that said it was "heavily guarded." None of the other rooms had anything like that in their descriptions, which led Steven and Brooklyn to deduce that the inventions were being held there.

Memorizing the location on the map, the duo hurried up a flight of stairs and stopped at the second level. They made their way through the cylinder-shaped corridor but froze when they turned the corner. A massively intricate laser grid spread down the rest of the hall, preventing Steven and Brooklyn from entering.

"What happens if something touches the lasers?" asked Brooklyn.

Steven investigated for a minute before responding. "Judging by the alarm on the other side, I think it's fair to say that the lasers are nonlethal. I'm sure touching them only sets off the alarm to alert the guard."

"Well, that's better than getting sliced," said Brooklyn casually.

"Ditto," Steven agreed. "I really wasn't looking forward to going home looking like a pack of deli meat. Let's try to find an off switch or something. It would be too easy if it were on *our* side of the hall."

It didn't take long for Brooklyn to discover the switch on the other side of the laser grid. One button was green, with the word "ON" pasted on the front. The other was red, bearing the word "OFF."

"I see it!" said Brooklyn, pointing it out. "The switch!"

"How do we reach it?" Steven wondered aloud.

Brooklyn snapped her fingers. "Leave that to me!" she said.

Brooklyn activated one of her Element Blasters and formed a long thin pole made of silicone. It was about fifteen feet long, but the good news was that it didn't weigh much and was easy for her to pick up. As carefully as she could, Brooklyn slipped the pole between the lasers to the other side of the hall where the switch was. Finally, she jammed the rod against the off switch, and the lasers disappeared immediately.

"Piece of cake," said Brooklyn as she put the pole down on the floor along the wall.

"Nice work," Steven said.

They continued down the hall at a brisk pace, making a left at the corner and then a right.

They were now in a very long, windowless corridor that was wider than it was tall. Nothing seemed out of the ordinary at first, as the room was totally empty, but Steven and Brooklyn were smart and moved steadily through the corridor, staying alert as they looked in all directions.

All directions except for the *floor*, that is. They hadn't realized that they had stepped on a flat camouflaged panel, stretching across the floor from one wall to another as if to ensure that whoever entered the hall stepped on it.

There was a sudden snap that sounded like a bolt lock sliding out of place. Another panel, the size of a lunchbox, slid open on the wall, and a miniature cannon emerged. Unexpectedly, the tip of the cannon began to glow a blinding yellow. Knowing it

THE TABLE OF ELEMENTS AND THE SPACE STATION OF SRILVAKOR | 111

most likely meant danger, Steven and Brooklyn reacted quickly and ran down the hall as soon as the cannon fired its ammo, which was a laser. When the laser hit the floor, it instantly solidified into a cage made of pure plasma.

As Steven and Brooklyn continued to run, more panels along the wall opened, and more cannons emerged, blasting more plasma cages at them. The duo ran even faster, and Steven was having a hard time keeping track of how many cannons were firing at them, but he was sure it was at least sixteen.

As if things couldn't get worse, the massive steel door at the end of the hall began to close. As fast as they could, Steven and Brooklyn slid under the door the moment before it sealed itself shut with an air-tight hiss.

On the other side of the door was the second largest room in the entire station, after the foyer. The room was a complete square and on the back wall, about sixty feet away, was a row of empty escape pods ready for launch. About fifty feet ahead was a three-foot-high brick-shaped box, made of metal, and sitting on a pedestal, just as Mr. Gargon described. They had reached the inventions! Now all they had to do was walk over and open the box.

"Wait a minute," said Brooklyn. "This seems way too easy. Isn't there supposed to be a guard?"

Oh, no. Steven had completely forgotten. Was Tyler Tarsus about to show up and fight them? Just as he was thinking this, a loud hiss interrupted the stillness, and an enormous futuristic door to their right shot up into the ceiling. Steven's heart skipped a beat. He could hear someone running, and an unidentified shadow grew closer at a frighteningly quick pace. The hairs on Steven's arms stood up as his insides went cold with fear. The guard was entering the room.

CHAPTER TWELVE

T HE GUARD WASN'T Tyler Tarsus after all. It was a skinny, bespectacled teenage girl with green skin, curly purple hair that reached her waist, and a lab coat. Steven thought she looked like a live-action version of a cartoon character. She came scampering into the room and stopped when she was in front of the pedestal.

"Did I miss my cue? Sorry!" she said as she gasped for breath, clutching her chest and pushing her futuristic-looking spectacles back up her nose. She had an energetic high-pitched voice. "I don't really run. Maybe I should get an elliptical for the station. Or a treadmill."

Steven and Brooklyn stared at the girl curiously. Steven assumed she was an alien, but why she was here was a mystery.

"It's rude to stare at someone," said the girl.

"Sorry," said Steven.

"You've never seen an alien before?" the girl asked.

"No," Steven answered. "But I've always wanted to!"

"Oh, thank you. You flatter me," the alien replied with a slight grin.

"So, you're the guard?" Brooklyn asked.

"Yes, yep, yes ma'am, I am!" said the alien happily. She smiled so wide that she looked like a frog. "Well, *temporarily* at least. The *real* guard is busy spending quality time with his loving wife on the planet Cranvulu. I'm just filling in for him because that's how sweet a gal I am! I'm Donna! I'm fifteen years old and I shall be your *substitute* guard for today!" she announced overdramatically.

Steven, who had expected the alien to have a much more interesting name, was confused by the ubiquitous name she had. How a name like "Donna" was present in another galaxy was a mystery to him. Steven wanted to ask her about this, but he didn't know if Donna would find it rude. So instead, he asked, "Why are you holding a stick?"

"It's my weapon," Donna answered.

"Your *weapon?*" Brooklyn repeated. "Why does it have a marshmallow on top?"

"I was eating my snack when I heard you enter," Donna explained. "It's rude to interrupt someone." She laughed very childishly.

Brooklyn eyed the marshmallow closely. "It's not roasted," she pointed out.

"Oh, I have pyrophobia, so I eat them raw," Donna said before eating the marshmallow right off the stick. "I don't want to get burned by accident," she added while eating more marshmallows from a bag she pulled out of her pocket. "It's rude to ask someone too many questions."

"It's also rude to talk with your mouth full," said Steven

coolly. Wearing a slight sneer and crossing his arms, he stared at Donna with half-opened eyes.

Donna stopped eating at once. Brooklyn forced back a laugh.

Soon, Donna's goofy smile returned.

"All right, all right," said Donna. "I'll give you that one. You guys may be tough, but there's no way you're getting these inventions."

"We're only here to return them to a friend," said Brooklyn.

Donna looked shocked, then laughed again. "Oh, *ho!* So *that's* who you're working for! Well, I'm sorry, but these will be staying right here in that pretty little case," she said, pointing to the inventions with her thumb over her shoulder. "So, what are we waiting for? Let's start the game!"

"'Game?'" Steven repeated, raising a brow.

"Your job is to get the inventions," Donna explained. "My job is to *keep you* from getting the inventions. Do we understand?"

Steven and Brooklyn stared at each other, brows raised and expressions bearing immense confusion.

"Great! Now come and get them!" said Donna. She defensively held her stick in the air and yodeled a goofy battle cry.

Steven felt like laughing. He was pretty sure he and Brooklyn would easily be able to get by a guard whose only weapon was a little stick and who had the mental maturity of a kindergartener. Calmly, the duo started for the case.

"Let's get this over with," said Steven.

"Tut, tut, tut!" Donna sang. "What fun is a game if it's too easy?"

She jumped up and smacked a button on the side of the wall with the back of her hand.

Steven and Brooklyn froze as the floor beneath them rumbled and shook like an earthquake. Steadily, large metal pillars rose from the floor, transforming the ball-field-sized room into a maze.

"Now it's even more fun!" Donna shouted from somewhere in the labyrinth.

Steven and Brooklyn stopped where they were, not sure what to expect next.

"Find me if you can!" Donna sang, her voice echoing throughout the room.

"Let's split up," Steven whispered to Brooklyn. "It'll be harder for her to catch both of us."

Quickly but quietly, Steven headed down the right path and Brooklyn down the left. He was surprised by how many turns and dead ends were in the maze, and he couldn't fly over the pillars because they rose to the ceiling without even a half-inch of space.

Just then, he thought he heard something. Steven stood silently with his back and arms pressed against a wall, trying to hear where Donna was. Suddenly … *POOF!* Donna instantly appeared in front of him in a puff of smoke. Before Steven could cry out in shock, Donna smacked him with a pillow and laughed flightily before throwing a large smoke pellet at the floor. She disappeared from view.

"What just happened?" said Steven, trying to process the strange event.

Donna appeared behind him almost instantly. "Teleportation! *Round two!*" She smacked Steven with the pillow again and, using another smoke pellet, disappeared before Steven could catch her.

"Just kidding!" Donna's voice called out from an unknown

spot in the maze. "Smoke pellets! Besides my exquisite humor, I greatly pride myself on my stealth skills!"

"What happened to your stick?" said Steven.

"Pillows are softer! I don't want to hurt my new playmates!" Donna remarked, her voice echoing.

"Silicon!" Steven hollered as he hurried through more of the labyrinth. "She has smoke pellets! Be alert!"

"Aah!" He heard Brooklyn yell, followed by more laughter. Donna must have gotten to her.

"This is so weird!" said Brooklyn, sounding annoyed.

"Oh, no!" said Donna in a bubbly tone. "Pillow fights are fun!"

Donna yodeled again as the sound of another smoke pellet filled the room. "It's like a slumber party!" she cried.

Steven stopped again as he reached another corner of the maze. He needed to think of a plan. How would he and Brooklyn get to the inventions if Donna could seemingly appear wherever they were? Donna must have known every route in the maze like the back of her hand.

That's when Steven got an idea. If he could put out the lights, and make the room dark enough, then Donna wouldn't be able to find him and Brooklyn. Not only that but Steven and Brooklyn would still be able to see, thanks to their night vision. Steven was about to tell Brooklyn to put out the lights where she was, but he stopped himself. If he told her that, then Donna would hear it, too, and go out of her way to ensure they wouldn't do that. Donna might have been goofy and childish, but she also seemed very cunning.

Steven might not have been able to fly over the maze, but he could still fly all the same. As silently as he could, Steven hovered to the ceiling. Then, he flipped himself upside down and slammed his foot into the light. The little area he was in went dark immediately, but at that point, he realized that he hadn't exactly thought his plan all the way through. Firstly, he had only damaged one light, and there must have been at least eight to ten more throughout the room. Secondly, the sound of breaking glass would not escape the notice of Donna, but Steven could still use this to his benefit.

Steven immediately hid behind one of the maze corners. Sure enough, Donna arrived at the scene at once through a trapdoor and seemed confused when she couldn't find Steven. Seizing the opportunity, Steven tiptoed out of sight before Donna could notice. As he turned another corner, he came face to face with Brooklyn. Both of them gasped at the unexpected sight of each other. Their faces grew red.

"Uh …" they both stammered, but they were too loud.

Donna appeared in a puff of smoke and cried, *"Aha!"*

But Steven and Brooklyn were prepared this time. Steven quickly snatched the pillow from Donna and tucked it under his arm while Brooklyn glued Donna's feet to the floor with two quick blasts of silicone.

With Donna restrained, Steven and Brooklyn ran through the rest of the maze together. Turning one last corner, they finally made it to the end. The case that housed Mr. Gargon's inventions was right in front of them.

Steven pressed the same button that Donna pressed earlier and deactivated the maze. The room returned to its normal state in a matter of seconds. Donna was still stuck in the silicone puddle, attempting to no avail to pull her feet out. As she was doing this, Brooklyn pulled a small lever on the side of the pedestal, releasing the box from the restraints that were holding it down.

"Mission accomplished," said Brooklyn with a cool grin as she hoisted the box and tucked it under her arm.

"Now that's what I'm talking about!" said Steven, high-fiving her.

It was then that Donna finally freed herself from the silicone and took a few steps toward Steven and Brooklyn. Even though her arms were crossed, she didn't look angry. On the contrary, she appeared to be in a good mood. Her goofy grin was still present, but her purple eyebrows were lowered, giving her a more casual expression.

"All right … you win," she said nonchalantly. "Good game. Very good, indeed."

"Tip of advice, Donna," said Steven, motioning to the pillow under his arm. "If you fight with *linen,* you're not *winnin'!*"

Steven thought he could hear crickets chirping.

"OK, that sounded a million times better in my head," he said embarrassedly.

"Maybe we should start practicing our one-liners," Brooklyn suggested.

"Sure. I'm… *down,*" said Steven with a grin, pointing to the pillow again.

"It's stuffed with cotton," said Brooklyn, noticing a rip in the pillow.

"This is not my day, is it?" said Steven disappointedly as he set the pillow down. A part of him feared more half-baked puns might come to him the longer he held it.

"Well, this has been fun," said Donna calmly. "Now, why don't you give me back that box and kindly tell me how you got those outfits."

"What?" Steven asked.

"Those suits belong to a friend of my parents—Helium, from the Table of Elements," said Donna. "How did you get them? Did you steal them? Are you taking them out for a joyride or something?"

Steven was completely puzzled. Donna's parents were friends of his father? How could someone guarding stolen property for a band of astronaut-thieves be the daughter of Boaz's friends?

"How do you know Helium?" Steven asked.

"How do *you* know him?" Donna reiterated.

"He gave us these suits," said Brooklyn. "We're good guys."

"You? Good guys?" Donna fell to the floor and clutched her stomach. She kicked her feet in the air like she was a swimmer, laughing hysterically. "If you're good guys, then why are you working with *Tyler Tarsus?*" she asked, wiping a tear from her eye.

Steven was the most confused he had been in a long time. Donna was an ally of the Table of Elements? And why did she think he and Brooklyn were working with Tyler Tarsus?

"What are you talking about?" said Steven. "We're helping Reginald Gargon get his inventions back. He told us that they were stolen from him by a group of astronauts!"

Donna raised a brow. "Who is Reginald Gargon?" she asked.

Steven stared at Brooklyn, feeling dreadfully confused. She stared at him, too. From the look on her face, she was just as baffled as he was.

Suddenly, there was a noise that sounded like a puff of smoke and a quick grunt from Donna. Steven and Brooklyn spun around and discovered Donna unconscious on the floor, snoring slightly. And right behind her was Mr. Gargon, holding a blaster Steven assumed was loaded with sleeping gas.

Before the duo could say or do anything, Mr. Gargon lunged at them and snatched the box out of Brooklyn's hands.

"What are you—?!" Brooklyn started.

Mr. Gargon swept Steven and Brooklyn's feet with his leg

and knocked them to the floor before he pried open the box and pulled out the inventions. They were two armored gloves with spray nozzles on top and buttons on the index fingers— *Element Blasters.*

Mr. Gargon slipped on an Element Blaster, aimed the nozzle at Steven and Brooklyn, and pressed the index finger button with his thumb. A strange silver substance exploded out of the nozzle, not quite liquid but not entirely solid either. Immediately, Steven and Brooklyn were trapped back to back in a tight titanium shell, leaving only their heads and necks exposed. They looked like butterflies poking their heads out of a silver cocoon.

"Mr. Gargon! What are you doing?" Steven exclaimed in complete shock.

"How did you get in here?" said Brooklyn. "You told us there was a forcefield."

"I just made that up." Mr. Gargon scoffed as he put on the other Element Blaster. "If you knew I could enter myself, you would have questioned why I desired your help. And don't bother trying to free yourselves. That shell I encased you in is solid titanium, two inches thick. My Element Blasters still work as they did before."

"'Titanium?'" said Brooklyn.

"'Element Blasters?'" said Steven. "Those are what you invented?"

"I did nothing of the sort," said Mr. Gargon calmly. "The Table of Elements are the true constructors, but they did build them for *me.* Little did they know I had other plans for them. The hero route seemed quite lackluster and disinteresting. I thought the *villain* route would be more … *amusing.*"

"Wait a minute," said Steven. He had just put two and two together. "You're … *You're Tyler Tarsus!*"

"Bingo," said Tarsus slowly with an evil grin.

"You *lied* to us?" said Brooklyn. "I thought … I thought we were friends!"

"Of course, I lied!" snapped Tarsus. "It was all an act. I knew who you were the whole time … *Steven and Brooklyn!*" He addressed them with an evil sneer. "Why else do you think I seemed so intrigued when you told me your last name, Steven?"

Steven and Brooklyn stared in horror. A villain knew who they really were, and not just any villain, but the most *infamous* villain in all of San Francisco. What would he do with this knowledge now that he had it? Steven fearfully wondered.

"When Boaz jettisoned me into space all those years ago," said Tarsus, "I accidentally set off the hyper-sleep system while attempting to take control of the pod. It wasn't until an asteroid hit it nearly thirteen years later that I awoke and finally managed to do so.

"As soon as I took control, I flew back to this station to retrieve the Element Blasters, only to find that Donna's father guarded them with several defense systems that had been set up in my absence. I was unprepared to complete the task, so I returned to Earth, hid in that abandoned 'hill-house' in San Francisco, and spent two months building various devices to aid my conquest. One night, as I was halfway through constructing my spaceship, I was rummaging through different dumpsters throughout the city, looking for metal and tools. It just so happened that I was rummaging through the dumpster behind City Hall the very night you two were deputized, and I overheard everything through the window.

"When I found out that there were new crime fighters in town, I used the two robots I had built to test your powers. Seeing that you were as skilled as I feared, I knew I had to get you out of San Francisco so I could carry out my plan. Since I knew your identities, I was able to find out which school you attended. So I snuck into Pine Tree High last night and flooded the place to make sure you had the day off. That way, you would be able to patrol the city again, find me in the Bay, and come with me here. It worked just as I planned, and now that you're here, all trapped and helpless, the only things left to mark off on my little checklist are 'get rid of you' and 'take over the city.'"

"'Get ... *rid of us?*'" Steven managed to say, feeling cold at the thought.

Tarsus grabbed the end of the titanium shell and dragged the kids across the room to the escape pods behind the empty case. The shell scraped the floor along the way. Steven realized what was about to happen even before Tarsus dropped him and Brooklyn on their sides inside one of the pods. Pressing a few buttons, the pod went dark as it sealed itself shut and blasted into space. As if things weren't bad enough, the hyper-sleep system engaged, spraying sleeping gas into the pod. Steven tried to fight it—to stay awake—but it was like trying to wade through cement.

"Father," Steven prayed, "please forgive me for helping Tyler Tarsus. I'm so sorry for being prideful and for all the sinful things I've done. I'm sorry that I dragged Brooklyn into this, too. If You're willing, please help us, Father. Please!"

Then, after failing to resist the sleeping gas, Steven and Brooklyn closed their eyes and fell fast asleep. They were now stranded in the middle of space, lightyears from home, with no one to rescue them.

* * *

As for Tyler Tarsus, he was as happy as could be. He was finally reunited with his beloved Element Blasters and had disposed of the new heroes lickety-split. His evil plan was almost complete. All he had left to do was to return to Earth and take over San Francisco.

But on his way back through the corridors, a strange feeling came over him. He remembered walking these very halls with the four heroes he used to call friends. He remembered how fun those times had been.

No. What was he thinking? He was getting distracted. The more he pondered it, the longer it would take for him to return to Earth to carry out his scheme.

But then, he discovered the very room where he had first been given the titanium Element Blasters. The very table that he and the original Table of Elements stood around was still there as though time hadn't passed. Images flashed in his head of that day—of the party decorations, the cake, the punch, and … his friends. The very friends whom he jettisoned into space … in a pod that exploded.

"*No!*" he thought to himself. "Stop it! You have a city to take over!"

And he refused to dwell more on the past and his old friends. "*No!*" he said again. He was a villain, and villains had no friends. He returned to his spaceship and blasted off back to Earth. San Francisco would soon be his, and without Steven and Brooklyn, there would be no one to stop him.

CHAPTER THIRTEEN

"WAKE UP! WAKE up!" said a muffled voice.

Everything looked and sounded like it was underwater. Steven could hardly make out what was happening.

"Wake up! Wake up!" repeated the voice, sounding clearer now.

At last, all the blurriness had gone away, and Donna the alien had come into focus. She was standing over Steven with a small bottle of smelling salts.

Steven sat up at once and noticed Brooklyn sitting beside him, also awake and unharmed. The titanium shell that previously trapped them had been removed and was resting in the corner of the ... *space station?*

The three of them were in the room where Tyler Tarsus's Element Blasters had been held. Steven was as perplexed as could be. He thought he and Brooklyn had been jettisoned in an escape pod by Tarsus. How were they back here? Had the whole thing been a dream?

"Donna?" said Steven cautiously. "H-how did we get here? What happened?"

"I went to the control room and rerouted the trajectory of the escape pod," Donna replied. "Welcome back!"

"Why would you do that? I thought we were your enemies."

"Enemies? Oh no!" Donna said with a laugh. "I admit, I tried to stop you from getting the Element Blasters because I thought you were villains yourselves. But after Tarsus knocked me out, I watched the footage from the surveillance cameras to see what had happened while I was unconscious. When I saw how shocked you were when Tarsus trapped you and stole the Element Blasters, I realized you had no idea he was evil. So, I remotely reset the escape pod you were in to bring you back to the station.

"Now before you say, 'Why didn't Boaz use that when Tarsus's escape pod went missing years ago,' it's because my parents didn't make those upgrades until *after* it happened. Anyway, when you came back, I cut you out of that metal cocoon and grabbed some smelling salts to wake you up from hyper-sleep. It's a good thing I was able to shut down the hyper-sleep system as soon as I did. If I had stayed in that pod a few seconds longer while I was getting you out, I definitely would have fallen asleep, too, and then we'd *all* be in trouble! And I got to admit, it wasn't easy finding something sharp enough to slice through solid titanium, but I managed all the same."

There was a pause. Steven thought the explanation was long and confusing.

"Oh," he said simply.

"How long have we been out?" Brooklyn asked.

Donna pulled a small bronze disk out of her lab coat pocket.

When she clicked a button on the side, a light blue hologram emerged from the center of the emblem, revealing the time.

"About forty-five minutes," Donna answered. "Tarsus took the spaceship. No doubt he's long gone by now."

"I don't understand. Reginald Gargon looks nothing like Tyler Tarsus!" said Steven. "My dad showed me a picture of him last week. He only had a mustache, not a beard. And he was *blond*."

"After he woke up from hyper-sleep, he must have dyed his hair to prevent anyone in San Francisco from recognizing him, including you two," said Donna.

"That explains why he always wore loose-fitting clothes," said Steven. "To hide his physique."

"Why did he use the hyper-sleep feature on us?" Brooklyn asked. "Why didn't the pod explode?"

"After the terrible events that happened all those years ago, Boaz asked my parents to disable the self-destruct feature from all the pods for safety reasons," Donna explained. "He didn't want to risk anyone else being destroyed the same way his friends were."

"And how do you know my dad?" Steven asked.

"It's an intriguing tale of friendship and an occupation born out of it!" said Donna. "My parents built this space station a little while before I was born. They were astronomers and inventors, and they gave the kind gentlemen, Boaz Starcluster, and his team, permission to use the station if they ever needed a break from city life.

"One day, Boaz and his pals held a meeting up here with their new recruit, Tyler Tarsus. From what my mom told me, the Table of Elements were going to make Tarsus an official member of their team—a superhero, like them—and had even built him his own Element Blasters. But Tarsus betrayed the team and killed all of them except for Boaz. After Boaz defeated Tarsus and sent him out in an escape pod, my parents tended to Boaz's injuries and cooked for him during the few days he was here. After he recovered, Boaz told my parents that he had a son to return to in a place called 'San Frantristco.'"

"San Fran-*cis*-co," Brooklyn politely corrected.

"Thanks," said Donna. "So, on the day he left, Boaz gave my parents the titanium Element Blasters and asked if they could guard them. Since the three of them were such close friends, my parents agreed to the task, and Boaz returned to Earth, alone, after a final farewell. I was only a toddler when I met him, so I don't remember him much. But I *do* remember that he was very kind despite the loss he endured."

"Do you live here? On this station?" Brooklyn asked.

"Yeah," said Donna, much more cheerfully. "Coolest house in the world! I mean, 'the galaxy!'"

"Where are your parents?" asked Steven.

"Gathering food on another planet," Donna replied. "They should be back in a few days, but they left me in charge in the meantime. You're the first visitors I've had all week … you and *Tarsus*."

"He's probably back in San Francisco by now," said Brooklyn, sounding worried. "We need to get down there and stop him or innocent people could die!"

Steven felt terrible. How could he have let Tarsus trick him? Steven knew that if anything happened to the city and its citizens, it would be all his fault for unintentionally aiding a supervillain in his evil scheme.

"I don't know how we're going to stop him," he told Brooklyn. "He must have taken the spaceship, and I don't think the escape pods can get us there in time."

"Actually, they can!" said Donna. "I modified them in my

spare time after the reroute feature was added. The pods will be able to take you to Earth in less than ten minutes!"

"Perfect. Thanks!" said Brooklyn.

"No problem, new friend," said Donna. "I wish you the best, and may God be with you."

"You don't want to come with us?" said Steven.

"I would, but I don't want my parents to worry in case they come home early," Donna explained.

"Fair enough," said Steven. "Thanks for your help."

"Anytime, Mr. Boaz's son," said Donna, resuming her goofy grin as she over-dramatically saluted.

Steven and Brooklyn climbed into the nearest escape pod after Donna instructed them on how to work the launch settings inside. Saying one last goodbye, Brooklyn twisted the hatch door shut as Steven activated the launch protocol. Thirty seconds later, they soundlessly blasted off into space with its coordinates set for San Francisco.

CHAPTER FOURTEEN

AT FIRST, STEVEN thought that Tarsus's spaceship had been fast, but that was nothing compared to how fast the *escape pod* was. Donna was certainly an exceptional engineer like her parents. In less than ten minutes, the pod entered Earth's atmosphere and deployed a massive parachute, causing the contraption to gently splash into the San Francisco Bay and float on top of the water.

Steven kicked the hatch door open and flew him and Brooklyn to the boardwalk.

"Hey, we're not far from where we first went on patrol," Brooklyn pointed out as she and Steven started down the sidewalk.

Several cars drove by so fast that they sounded like roaring tigers. Bags and luggage were tied to the tops of the cars as they made their way west, probably to the Golden Gate Bridge. Steven assumed an evacuation was occurring.

"Excuse me, ma'am?" Steven asked a woman who was passing by with a large suitcase. "What's going on?"

"A man in a giant robot has invaded the city!" the woman cried in a trembling voice as she placed her suitcase into the trunk of her car. "He's heading for City Hall. He said that he's going to hold the mayor and the city officials hostage until he's named ruler!"

Steven went cold with fear. He hoped it wasn't too late. "How far is he from City Hall?" he asked, hoping there was still time.

"Probably more than halfway by now. His suit can walk just as fast as my car can drive, and it can even jump over a two-story building! I saw him do it myself!"

"Continue evacuating," Brooklyn ordered. "We'll take it from here."

The woman nodded before climbing into her car and driving off.

Steven pulled out his phone and called Boaz to make sure he was OK. To his relief, Boaz said that he was safe in the penthouse.

"I tried calling you earlier but couldn't get a signal," said Boaz.

"We were in space," said Steven awkwardly.

"'Space?'"

"It's a long story."

"You can tell me later. Save the mayor."

Steven hung up, then sprayed helium on Brooklyn. The two of them soared above the rooftops until they arrived at the corner of Poke and McAllister, just outside San Francisco City Hall.

Tarsus was indeed inside a giant mech-suit, just like the woman said. The suit was about eighty feet tall, sixty feet wide, and coated with a thick layer of titanium. Its body was shaped like a brick, and Tarsus controlled the mech by sitting in the very center of the body. The mech-suit had no head, but it did have massively long arms; huge, clenched titanium fists; long, strong legs; and colossal titanium feet. The ground shook and rumbled with each movement Tarsus's mech-suit made.

"How did he build that so fast?" Brooklyn wondered after she and Steven landed.

"I don't think he *did* build it so fast," said Steven. "I saw a giant exoskeleton in his garage near the spaceship. He must have made that in the two months he spent preparing and then coated it with titanium from the Element Blasters today."

Tarsus aimed his giant metal fists in the direction of City Hall, and Steven and Brooklyn knew they had to act quickly, or the people inside could be harmed or even killed.

"Tarsus!" Steven hollered. "We're down here! Leave the building alone!"

Tarsus turned around so fast that his mech made a whooshing noise. He looked like he had just seen a cow fly.

"How did you get here?" he shouted with a puzzled expression.

Apparently, the suit was equipped with a powerful microphone that allowed everyone on street level to hear him as though he *wasn't* several yards above the ground.

"We had a little help from our new friend," said Steven.

"Stop what you're doing this minute, Tarsus!" Brooklyn shouted. "We don't want to fight you. We'd rather talk this out."

"We have nothing to talk about!" Tarsus said with a growl.

Suddenly, the panels in the mech's legs slid open. Four tall robots, with their arms stretched out as if they were ready to snatch something from a windowsill, galloped out of each leg toward Steven and Brooklyn.

"Destroy them!" Tarsus ordered the robots.

"I'll take care of the bots!" Steven told Brooklyn. "You get everyone out of the building!"

"On it!" said Brooklyn. She immediately hurried to the City Hall building and blasted silicone at the hands of Tarsus's mechsuit, binding them together. She also glued his mechanical feet to the pavement. As the villain struggled to free himself, Brooklyn flung open the door to the Hall and dashed inside as fast as she could, but not before shielding the front of the building with a layer of silicone for extra precaution.

While she was inside, Steven stayed occupied on the street and battled the robots. He pulled one of the bots in half by using his helium as though two invisible people had been tugging on either side. Next, he blasted helium on another, sending it high into the air before dropping it from about a hundred feet, causing it to crumble on impact. Steven then flew between the remaining pair, sprayed them, spun them midair, and slammed them into the street.

Just then, Tarsus broke free of his silicone restraints and stomped toward Steven like a gorilla awakened from its slumber. He reached his hands down and swung at Steven as though he were a fly. When he missed, he tried to step on him. Steven zigzagged a few feet off the ground, avoiding Tarsus's attacks and keeping the villain occupied while Brooklyn led everyone from City Hall away from the battle as quietly as possible.

Unfortunately, Tarsus took his eyes off Steven and noticed the mayor and the others escaping. He growled as he blasted a large blob of titanium at the group, which instantly solidified into a cage around the terrified mayor and the other politicians. Tarsus started stomping toward them, so Steven quickly fired helium at the back of the giant mech and pulled as hard as he could. Tarsus struggled to break free of the helium's power as Brooklyn, who climbed the side of the building, leaped off the roof wearing a giant silicone block as a glove. Steven assumed that she was trying to use it to break off the mech's arm or something, but he never found out because Tarsus smacked Brooklyn aside with the back of his hand. Brooklyn's armor protected her from the blow. She created a silicone firefighter pole and slid down to the street.

Tarsus spun around and kicked Steven away, but in midair, he powered his Helium Boots before he could hit the ground. Tarsus was about to do the same to Brooklyn, but Steven sprayed her with helium and swiftly pulled her out of the way and over to where he was.

"Thanks," said Brooklyn as she stood beside him.

"No prob," said Steven quickly.

Burning with rage, Tarsus picked up a car and threw it at the duo. Steven instantly sprayed the car with helium and threw it back at the villain, hoping it might take out the mech's legs, but Tarsus jumped at the last second, and the car kept flying until it smashed into another vehicle. To Steven's horror, someone had been standing beside it. He wasn't hurt, but he looked horrified at the sight.

"My car!" he cried.

"Argh!" Steven screamed through gritted teeth. That man's car had been destroyed all because of another mistake he made.

"Get out of here as far as you can!" Brooklyn ordered the man. *"Hurry!"*

The man obeyed at once, still looking sorrowful at the loss of his car.

Tarsus raised his fists as high as he could, and just when he was about to slam them down on Steven and Brooklyn, the latter activated her Element Blasters again and formed a thick silicone dome around her and Steven. It might have been dark inside, since the dome had no holes, but the heroes could still see perfectly thanks to their night vision.

Tarsus continued to strike the dome with his fists, but the structure would not break. Inside, Steven and Brooklyn caught their breaths.

"OK. We're OK," said Brooklyn in a low voice.

She paused, listening to the muffled thuds of the dome being pounded by Tarsus's giant fists. "The dome won't hold forever," she said. "We need to be prepared for when it breaks."

But when she turned around, she noticed that Steven was just sitting there with his head down, not looking the least bit prepared for battle.

"Dude, come on!" said Brooklyn. "I need your help."

"I can't help you," said Steven miserably. "I'd probably just make things worse."

Brooklyn looked confused. "Why are you saying that?" she said in a tone of concern. "What's wrong?"

Steven knew he could tell Brooklyn the truth. He sighed. "After the school bus incident, I felt terrible because I knew everyone on that bus suffered because of something *I* did. Everyone was still angry at me when we went back to school, and I got punched in the face. No one had forgiven me, and I knew no one would *ever* forgive me unless I made it up to them. I wanted to do that by being a hero to the city, saving people's lives, and helping them with their problems. I hoped that they would finally admit just how wrong they were and accept me as a changed person. Then, I messed up again. I told you to go into space with me and someone we hardly knew, and now, Tarsus has the Element Blasters back, the mayor and the rest of City Hall are in a cage, and it's all my fault! Everything

I've done in these past two weeks has made people miserable! I should just return my license to your dad. I don't deserve it."

Steven sniffled and began to cry. Despite all the commotion outside, Brooklyn leaned over and hugged him tightly. Steven hugged her back.

"I'm a failure!" he cried.

"*Steven,*" said Brooklyn softly. "You're not a failure. You're my best friend."

"But—"

"I want you to answer some questions for me," Brooklyn interrupted.

Steven paused, sniffling one last time before saying, "OK."

"Are you sorry for the bad things you've done?" Brooklyn asked.

"Yes," Steven answered.

"Did you ever ask God for forgiveness?"

Steven remembered when he was lying in bed at the hospital. He *had* asked God for forgiveness.

"Yes," he answered. "I did."

"Did you also ask God to forgive you for unintentionally helping a villain?"

"Yes," Steven replied.

"When you asked God for forgiveness, did you actually feel sorry for what you did, or did you just say words?"

"I … I was sorry," said Steven. "I really was. What I did hurt many people. I asked God to forgive me and help me do better."

"Most importantly, do you believe that Jesus is the Son of God and that He died for your sins?"

"Yes," said Steven confidently.

Brooklyn smiled. "Then guess what, Steven?" she said. "God has forgiven you."

"But-but all I did was pray to Him," Steven stammered. "How could He just forgive me without me doing anything to make up for it?"

"Because Jesus already took care of that more than two thousand years ago," Brooklyn explained. "When Jesus died on the cross, He took away all our sins and punishment so that we may live with Him forever in heaven. If we accept Jesus as Savior, He comes to live in us, and our sins are forgiven. 1 John 1:9 says it better than I ever could: 'If we confess our sins, He is faithful and just to forgive us our sins, and to cleanse us from all unrighteousness.'"

"But I don't *feel* forgiven," Steven admitted.

"I've been there, too," said Brooklyn. "So have *lots* of people. But God has forgiven you even if you don't feel it. Your problem isn't that you haven't been forgiven; your problem is that you haven't forgiven *yourself.*"

"'Myself?' " Steven repeated.

"It's one of the hardest things a person has to do," Brooklyn continued. "Your ego hurts, and you want people to view you positively. But you don't need their approval to be happy because God will love you no matter what you do. Now, that doesn't mean you can just go out and sin like there's no tomorrow. We still need to obey God, not because it will get us into heaven, but because we love Him and worship Him. We're saved by grace through faith. Once you accept God's grace, you are washed clean and no longer have to live with guilt and shame."

Steven said nothing. He pondered Brooklyn's words. His attempts to make up for the terrible things he had done were all for nothing. He had already been forgiven by God, and now he knew the truth.

"I'm forgiven," Steven said slowly and quietly. He smiled. "God is with me."

Brooklyn smiled with him. "God has blessed us with the mantle of the Table of Elements," she said. "Let's use our gifts to please *Him* instead of people."

Steven smiled wider. He felt like a weight had been lifted off his shoulders.

Suddenly there was a much louder thud on top of the dome. It seemed as though Tarsus's repeated hammer-fists were finally paying off. A crack was spreading through the top of the dome's interior, but Steven was not scared. He knew that he and Brooklyn could do anything with God on their side.

"Let's do this, partner," said Steven bravely.

Brooklyn grinned in a "let's get this party started" kind of way. "All right!" she exclaimed. "What's your plan?"

Steven looked down at the ground and discovered that they were sitting on top of a sewer lid. The plan came to him as quick as a flash.

"Follow me!" he said.

CHAPTER FIFTEEN

A S TARSUS CONTINUED to strike the outside of the dome, Steven, still inside it with Brooklyn, powered up his blasters and used an adequate amount of helium to lift the sewer lid out of its place. He threw the lid aside, and it fell to the street with a heavy clank. Then, Steven and Brooklyn leaped into the pitch-black tunnel with their masks once again providing them with night vision.

"Maybe this *wasn't* such a good idea," said Steven, wrinkling his nose at the filthy, dirt-colored water he was knee-deep in.

Despite the foul stench and the grime-covered environment, Steven and Brooklyn focused solely on saving the city and waded through the tunnel as fast as possible, unintentionally splashing water behind them.

Seconds later, they came to a ladder which led to another sewer lid. Considering the distance they traveled in such short a time, they were able to determine that they were close behind Tarsus. Steven and Brooklyn climbed the ladder and carefully slid the lid off the opening, exposing the duo to the partly cloudy afternoon sky.

As they climbed out, as quiet as field mice, they discovered that Tarsus had finally managed to break through the silicone dome. The base was still intact, but the top had been cracked and crushed into clay-like crumbles. Though they couldn't see his face, the duo figured that Tarsus was confused and furious to find that his nemeses had disappeared.

Steven silently flew him and Brooklyn to the cage that held the City Hall employees. Brooklyn stuck one of her Element Blasters between the bars and formed a large brick-like object. The longer she held the button on her index finger, the more the brick expanded until its mighty tensile strength pushed the bars open wide enough for the people inside to escape.

"Get out of here!" Brooklyn whispered to them. "We'll handle Tarsus."

The sounds of Brooklyn talking and the people clambering out of the cage and running off caught Tarsus's attention. The villain turned a complete one-eighty in his giant mech-suit and eyed the duo with an evil glare.

Steven and Brooklyn stood heroically in the middle of the street, with their shoulders back and their fists on their hips. They stared courageously at Tarsus while the wind blew through their hair.

"Surrender now, Tarsus," Brooklyn ordered.

"The mayor is safe, and the Hall has been evacuated," Steven continued. "You've lost."

Tarsus growled. "You insignificant little brats! You can't defeat me! You're just children! I'll destroy you like I did the original team!"

The duo was unmoved.

"You won't win, Tarsus. With God on our side, all things are possible," Steven declared with the utmost confidence.

"And we're not *just* children," Brooklyn added bravely. "We're the *Table of Elements.*"

With a fuming look, Tarsus formed an enormous club with one of his Element Blasters and swung it at Steven and Brooklyn with his mech's mammoth hands. Steven took to the skies, and Brooklyn jumped and somersaulted out of the way a moment before the club struck the street, sending cracks in every direction.

Tarsus frantically swung his club in the air at Steven, who dodged every blow as he attempted to blast helium on the club. But Tarsus's swinging was just as fast as Steven's aerobatics.

Down on the street, Brooklyn glued the mech's feet together, and the suit toppled over like a chopped tree. As Tarsus came tumbling down, Steven finally managed to snag the club and use his helium to place the weapon on the roof of a nearby building, far out of Tarsus's reach.

With Tarsus on the ground, Brooklyn hastily tried to bind him with strong silicone ropes, but Tarsus pushed himself back onto his feet with the palms of his hands. He stomped and swung his hands around, trying to catch, crush, or step on the duo. Just when Brooklyn was about to be grabbed by one of the mech-suit's hands, she jumped out of the way and grabbed Steven's wrist as he swooped down. The two soared higher and circled Tarsus's head as Steven thought of the next move.

"Glue his hands together!" he ordered Brooklyn.

Steven continued to circle the mech as Brooklyn sprayed silicone at Tarsus's metal wrists with her Element Blasters, but Tarsus's suit was too strong. The villain ripped through the silicone like it was silk and swung his fists in the air like he was shadowboxing.

Then, Steven let go of Brooklyn, who made a silicone slide to avoid getting hurt. She used a long silicone rope to trip the mech. Next, Steven lifted Tarsus into the air, using his helium, and spun him around while Brooklyn wrapped the mech-suit up as tight as a drum. Finally, Steven set the mech down on the ground, and it did not move at all. Tarsus seemed to be defeated at last.

"Whew!" Steven wiped his brow before humorously realizing that he wasn't able to since he was wearing a mask. Brooklyn laughed a little at this.

"Mr. Tarsus," said Steven in a much more serious tone, "you are under arr—"

But the mech leaped to its feet and tore through the silicone instantly. Tarsus growled and glared furiously at the duo with bulging eyes, overflowing with unbottled rage. He snatched Steven and Brooklyn and held them in his robot hands as tightly as he could.

"I … have … *had it with you!"* Tarsus roared so loudly that it made the Earth shake. "I will not have my plot ruined by two pathetic teenagers!"

Tarsus dropped Steven and Brooklyn on the street like they were pizza dough. Before the two of them could move, Tarsus used his Element Blasters to cover their legs with a long block of titanium. Just when the teens were about to fire their own Element Blasters, Tarsus covered those with restraints, too, cementing Steven and Brooklyn's forearms to the street.

"I'm done playing games! I'm going to destroy you, and I'm going to *like it!"*

Tarsus raised his mech-suit's enormous foot high into the air—right above Steven and Brooklyn.

"Tyler! Don't do it!" Steven yelled.

"I don't take orders from you, Helium!" growled Tarsus.

"Please … you don't … want to do this!" Brooklyn called out as she tried to free herself from her restraints.

"Why not?" Tarsus barked. "Because it's wrong? Because it'll hurt you? Nothing—and I mean *nothing*—will stop me from taking over the city!"

Tarsus gave the kids one last evil look.

"Goodbye, children …"

Baring a hideous grin, Tarsus raised his foot even higher.

Though he really wanted to, Steven couldn't move his arms and legs—neither could Brooklyn—with the titanium wrapped around them.

With his eyes squeezed shut, Steven prayed aloud, "Please God! We need Your help!"

"Please Father!" said Brooklyn. "Please help us!"

Steven knew that the giant foot would come down upon him and Brooklyn any second, and they would begin the next chapter of their lives. For what it was worth, he had lived a great life. An *amazing* life. He had been raised by the best father he could have asked for—a father who taught him to love and obey the Lord.

Steven and Brooklyn had managed to do some good in the brief time they bore the mantle of the Table of Elements, and they had fought courageously to the very end. As bad as things seemed, the two friends were happy to have each other. They kept their eyes clenched shut as they awaited the descent of Tarsus's giant foot.

*   *   *

But Tarsus froze. His eyes had fallen on the street before him. Memory swept into his head like a roaring wave on a beach. He could vividly see himself walking along that very street many years ago, with none other than Boaz, Andrea, Robert, and Charlotte. All five were having a pleasant morning walk, laughing at an amusing story Robert had just told them.

Then his mind wandered even further. Wedding bells rang in Tarsus's head as he reminisced about the wedding of Boaz and Andrea, with himself serving as best man. He could still smell the majestic scent of the flowers on display. He saw all five of them celebrating his birthday with pizza and root beer floats during a surprise party, eating corndogs at Pier 39, watching the fireworks during the Fourth of July at Crissy Field, and watching a heartwarming movie by the fire on Christmas.

Tarsus's eyes returned to the heroes trapped beneath his raised foot. Steven and Brooklyn were praying, and they looked completely frightened. Their eyes were squeezed shut as they lay on the street beneath their restraints, unable to escape.

"This is Steven," Boaz had said, holding up his newborn for Tarsus to see. "Say 'hi' to Tyler, Steven!"

Bundled up in a baby blue blanket, Steven smiled at Tarsus as though he had just seen the sunrise for the first time. Tarsus smiled back as Boaz handed his child back to Andrea, who said, "I can tell you two are going to be great friends someday."

"I hope so," said Tarsus.

He remembered the joy he felt seeing his best friend's child for the first time. It wasn't an act, and it wasn't forced. It was genuine joy. He had known that that child was something special. And now that very child was all grown up … and he was about to be squashed by Tarsus himself.

Tarsus thought he had a panic attack for a fraction of a second. A chill went through his entire nervous system. No! What was he doing? How could he do this?

He recalled that tragic day on Donna's parents' space station.

He had attacked the Table of Elements when they didn't even have their armor or Element Blasters to protect themselves. As if they weren't already defenseless enough, Tarsus had used his new titanium powers to encase Andrea, Robert, and Charlotte in a solid metal block as he had done to Steven and Brooklyn. Tarsus could still see the horrified, heartbroken faces of the heroes whom he had once been friends with.

"Please, Tyler!" they had cried. "Don't do this! We're your friends!"

Then, right when he was about to finish them off … they started praying. They prayed aloud to their God, begging Him to help them. And now, Steven and Brooklyn were doing the same thing.

Tarsus almost screamed in anguish. No! *No!* He couldn't do it again! *He couldn't!*

*   *   *

Steven, who had been expecting himself to be squashed into a puddle almost a minute ago, cautiously opened his eyes. Tarsus's glare left his face as he gently lowered his foot—not on top of Steven and Brooklyn—but next to his other foot instead. At first, Steven thought he was seeing things because Tarsus's eyes were tearing up. Then, Tarsus, still in his mech, moved closer to the duo.

"Why … why did you stop?" Steven asked weakly.

Tarsus was silent for what felt like hours. Finally, he said in a voice no louder than a whisper, "You prayed."

He paused again. *"They* prayed, too."

Tarsus reached down with his giant metal hands and ripped the titanium restraints off the heroes. Steven and Brooklyn's arms and legs were free again, but they did not run away. They stayed where they were, curious to see what Tarsus would say or do next. As they stood silently, Tarsus opened the hatch to his mech and hopped down onto the street.

"What's going on?" asked Brooklyn.

"You win," said Tarsus in a trembling voice. "Before I ... killed ... the Table of Elements," he explained, sounding uncomfortable at the very mention, "I saw them do ... the same thing. I was just about to kill them .... They pleaded with me and prayed aloud to their God. Something came over me, and I felt like I couldn't kill them right there. So, I let the pod do the dirty work. I ... I still caused their deaths, but I felt uncomfortable using my own two hands to commit such an act. Yet, I still killed them .... It's been thirteen years since I've called anyone my friend. They were the only ones I ever knew. Boaz. Andrea. Robert. Charlotte .... The Table of Elements."

"They were good people," said Steven.

"They were indeed," Tarsus agreed in a solemn tone. "I lost my only friends, and when I saw you praying—the two of you pleading ... the same way they did—I knew ... I knew I couldn't make the same mistake I made all those years ago. I'm sorry for what I did to you, Steven. It's my fault you have to spend the rest of your life without your mother. The Table of Elements were the only friends I ever had, and I took such a friendship for granted. I never really thought about it, but now that I'm here, I realize that being with them, playing games, going to the beach, camping with them, having barbeques, and making s'mores, are the happiest memories I have. I've made a mess of things. I was so blinded by my plan for power that I didn't realize how great a life I truly had—how wrong the things I've done are."

He paused as silent tears trickled down his face, wetting his beard. "I'm sorry. For everything," he said in a hoarse whisper.

"You don't have to forgive me. I just wanted you to know. I don't deserve your compassion."

Steven paused, too. He was still soaking in Tarsus's words. Then, he stepped closer and comfortingly put his hand on Tarsus's shoulder.

"You might have done terrible things, Tyler," he said, "but we forgive you anyway."

Tyler looked shocked. Tears continued to pour down his face. "Why?" he asked in a surprised voice.

Steven smiled. "Because that's what Jesus would want us to do. I've also done some terrible things and didn't expect to ever be forgiven for them, but I've learned something from my wonderful partner here," he explained, motioning to Brooklyn.

"What's that?" Tyler asked.

"God promises to always forgive you when you come back to Him and accept His Son as Savior," Steven answered.

Tyler wiped his eyes with his large fingers. "Boaz and his friends used to tell me about that stuff," he said, "about how a Perfect Creator and Loving Father gave up His One and Only Son to save us from sin. I just … I just never got into the whole thing."

"Would you like to?" Steven asked.

Tyler was silent for a moment. It didn't feel like something done for dramatic purposes. He genuinely seemed to be contemplating the offer.

"Are you saying," he began, "that your kindness, your forgiveness—everything that made the two of you who you are—came from Him?"

"That's right," said Brooklyn.

Tyler paused yet again, but it was shorter than before. "I am forty-three years old," he soon said in a much less sorrowful voice. "My life is halfway over, and I want to change and spend the second half wisely. If this Jesus of whom you speak is all-powerful and made you who you are, then I ... I wish to learn more about Him. But I don't know .... Do you believe that a God as great and loving as He is could ever forgive someone like me?"

Steven smiled even wider, for he already knew the answer to that. "I know that He can," he said. "Without a doubt."

Tarsus smiled back. His once sinister, evil eyes were now warm and full of hope. Even his tears looked warmer, as tears do when one cries in joy.

"Come on," Steven continued. "Let's go home. Then, we can give you a Bible and help you with your new life."

Steven was about to walk away, but Brooklyn stopped him.

"I think we should talk to the police first," she said.

Chief Adams himself had just arrived with three police cars following. The officers didn't look too happy to see Tyler, but Steven and Brooklyn explained everything to the Chief and told him how Tyler was remorseful for his actions.

"It's the truth, sir," Tyler interjected. "I deserve punishment for my crimes. I surrender as an honest man should."

Tyler took off his Element Blasters and dropped them to the ground. Steven confiscated them as Tyler bowed his head and held out his hands. The police pulled his arms behind his back and handcuffed him.

"Mr. Tarsus, you are under arrest for attempted murder, attempted kidnapping of the mayor and the other occupants of City Hall, and for destruction done to the city," Chief Adams declared. "You have the right to remain silent. Anything you say can and will be used against you in court. You have a right to an attorney. If you cannot afford an attorney, one will be appointed for you."

"Please, sir ... could I please have one more minute with Helium and Silicon?" Tyler pleaded.

Chief Adams glanced at Steven and Brooklyn, who mouthed "please" while nodding. The Chief sighed and told Tyler in a firm tone, "You've got thirty seconds."

The officers who held Tyler's arms turned him so he could face Steven and Brooklyn.

Tyler exhaled happily. "Thank you," he told the duo.

"I'm sorry," Steven said in a soft voice.

"No," said Tyler calmly. "I deserve to go to prison. I killed your mother and nearly killed the two of you."

"God saved us," said Brooklyn.

"And now He has saved *me*," Tyler added. "I promise I won't reveal your identities to anyone. And Helium, please tell your father that I'm sorry. Tell him that ... I hope he can forgive me."

"Of course," said Steven. "And Silicon and I will come visit you."

"We'll come to the trial, too," Brooklyn added. "We'll put in a good word for you and help you learn more about Jesus."

"Thank you," Tyler concluded, "for everything,"

With these words, Tyler's time to talk ran out, and the police escorted him away. Chief Adams approached Steven and Brooklyn.

"I'm proud of you two," he said quietly. "You're real heroes."

"Thanks, Dad," Brooklyn whispered.

"Thank you, sir," said Steven. "And about the Element Blasters ..." He held them up for the Chief to see before continuing in a whisper, "Would it be OK if I gave them back to my dad? Since he helped build them?"

"Go ahead and do that," Chief Adams whispered back. "Thanks again for the help."

Though saddened that Tyler would be going to prison,

Steven was still delighted knowing that God had saved not just him and Brooklyn, and not just the city, but the *villain* whom they had encountered, too.

Word of the events spread like wildfire. It was all over the news. Witnesses were interviewed. Some shared their trauma of the events, and others praised the new heroes for saving the mayor and their city. But as proud as the people of San Francisco were, no two people were prouder than Boaz and Chief Adams. They met up at the latter's apartment that evening for a celebratory dinner, where Steven and Brooklyn told them about everything that happened that day, from meeting Reginald Gargon and Donna to the space station obstacles to the redemption of Tyler Tarsus.

As pleased as Boaz was with Steven and Brooklyn's achievements, he refrained from smiling at any mention of Tyler. His often warm eyes seemed stricken with anger and misery. Steven thought this would be the case. Even though he told his dad that Tyler was sorry, Steven wasn't sure if Boaz would ever be able to forgive him, let alone rebuild his friendship with him. But Steven hoped he would. He believed Tyler when he said he had changed, and he couldn't wait for him and Brooklyn to share the gospel with him.

CHAPTER SIXTEEN

TUESDAY, MARCH 30TH

AROUND A QUARTER past six that morning, Steven got up, brushed his teeth, threw on his bathrobe and slippers, and, hoping not to disturb his dad, tiptoed downstairs. He made his way to the kitchen, made some toast, and spread marmalade on the bread as he quietly, with only the kitchen light on, read his book at the counter.

As Steven finished his first piece of toast, Boaz entered the kitchen, wearing slippers and a robe of his own. "Like father, like son," Steven thought.

"Good morning," said Boaz quietly.

"Morning, Dad," said Steven.

Seeing that his dad was up despite his tiptoeing, he jokingly remarked, "Guess I need to work on my ninja skills."

Boaz gave a brief chuckle. "What are you reading?"

"*Intermediate Chemistry Studies,*" Steven answered. "I wanted to reread it for science class."

"I see," Boaz replied. "But why this early? You don't have to get up until seven."

"I couldn't sleep," said Steven. "Things were on my mind."

"Are you going to be OK going to school?" Boaz asked. "Will you be fine being around the kids from the crash?"

Steven put down his book and gave his father his full attention. "Well, I've been praying about it," he answered.

"And?" asked Boaz.

Steven sighed. He rubbed his hair. "I'll admit, I'm still kind of nervous, but I've asked God to give me courage. Not to mention, He's also given me a great friend to be by my side."

"Well, I'm happy to hear that," said Boaz.

"Speaking of Brooklyn," Steven continued, "I talked with her yesterday during our battle with Tyler. She helped me realize that me being a superhero, and the stuff I did as a superhero, wasn't really me being a superhero at all."

Boaz raised a brow, looking half-confused, half-intrigued.

"Basically," Steven elaborated, noticing the perplexed look on his father's face, "I was only being a superhero to make up for the bad things I did and to get people, even God, to love and forgive me. But Brooklyn told me that God has already forgiven me because I asked Him for forgiveness, and I'm truly sorry for what I've done. God loves me regardless of my choices and, no matter what happens, He will always be there for me."

Boaz smiled. "I love you, Steven," he said.

"I like you, too, Dad," said Steven playfully.

Boaz laughed, almost taken aback. "Are you serious?" he said with the most surprised grin.

"I'm very fond of you, dear Father?" Steven jokingly suggested.

The two of them laughed some more.

"I love you, Dad," Steven finally said.

"Now that's more like it!" said Boaz, giving his son a big hug.

*　　　　　*　　　　　*

An hour into school, Steven could tell that things were different. No one stared at him, whispered behind his back, or said anything mean or hurtful. The only people who said anything to him at all that morning were Principal Sanchez and Mrs. Hildebrandt, who expressed that they were glad to see him fully recovered.

When the students were dismissed at noon, Steven went to his locker to grab his lunch. As he closed the door, clutching a large paper bag, he was stopped by someone he didn't have a very good history with.

"Hey, Steven," said Eddie Macaron. He had moved past the wheelchair and was now supporting himself on crutches.

Steven grew pale, but he kept his cool. "Hey, Eddie," he said as casually as he could.

Eddie inhaled through his teeth. He looked like he was struggling to put his thoughts into words. "Look, I just wanted to say that … about the cafeteria … and the bus … I … I shouldn't have hurt you like I did back there. You didn't mean to wreck the bus. It took me a while to accept that."

Steven was stunned. Had he misheard him? Was the guy who had been picking on him since middle school saying that he was sorry?

"Wait," said Steven, "you're really apologizing?"

"Yeah," Eddie insisted. "I was watching the news the other day—yesterday—you know, and I … uh … I saw this guy, Tyler

Tarsus, being arrested after the new Table of Elements helped save the city. He told the police that he was sorry for what he did. I realized that ... if someone as evil as him could see how wrong his choices were, then I should be able to see that seeking revenge was wrong, too."

"Wow, Eddie," Steven said, almost laughing in amazement, "that's ... that's, uh ... that's incredible."

"Thanks, man," said Eddie. "So, are we cool?"

Steven remembered all the years that Eddie Macaron had bullied him. He remembered being punched by one of his goons in the cafeteria. He remembered all the terrible things Eddie had done, and Steven had only one thing to say to him: "We're *totally* cool."

After the unexpected, yet wonderful, apology from Eddie, Steven met Brooklyn outside the cafeteria doors. The two of them entered and sat in the back corner of the room to talk in private.

"Eddie really apologized?" Brooklyn asked, sounding shocked.

Steven nodded. "Yeah," he said.

"That's amazing." Brooklyn paused. A look of concern appeared. "Did you tell him you're Helium?"

"No," Steven answered. "He doesn't need to know. God has already forgiven me, and that's what's important. It's like my dad said: 'A hero doesn't do things for personal gain, but to serve God and to help people.'"

"I'm proud of you, dude," said Brooklyn.

"And I'm proud of *you*," Steven added, "for sticking by my side, thick and thin."

Brooklyn beamed as the two turned their attention to their lunch bags.

"You know," Steven said, "I was thinking."

"Uh huh?" said Brooklyn.

"I still think it seems kind of weird calling ourselves the Table of Elements when there's only two of us."

"You think we should recruit new members?" Brooklyn asked.

"I've been considering it," Steven admitted. "It would be pretty sweet to have a full team someday, like the original Table of Elements. Maybe Donna will want to join."

"That would be cool," said Brooklyn. "But for now, I'm happy with it being just you and me."

Steven smiled. "Me, too," he said. "Helium and Silicon— *the Chemical Duo!* I can't wait to see how our journey grows."

"Neither can I, partner!" said Brooklyn. "Neither can I."

Printed in the United States
by Baker & Taylor Publisher Services